Eden's Escape

Eden's Escape

M. Tara Crowl

DISNEP • HYPERION
LOS ANGELES   NEW YORK

First Edition, September 2016
1 3 5 7 9 10 8 6 4 2
FAC-020093-16204

Printed in the United States of America
This book is set in Cochin
Designed by Phil Caminiti

Library of Congress Cataloging-in-Publication Data
Names: Crowl, M. Tara, author.
Title: Eden's escape / M. Tara Crowl.
Description: First edition. | Los Angeles : Disney-Hyperion, [2016] |
Series: Eden of the lamp ; 2 | Sequel to: Eden's wish | Summary: After
escaping her enchanted lamp, Eden begins a new life in Manhattan,
but the rebellious twelve-year-old genie only gets a taste of the
city's wonders before she is whisked away for a wish granting.
Identifiers: LCCN 2016006655 | ISBN 9781484711866 (hardback)
Subjects: | CYAC: Genies—Fiction. | Magic—Fiction. | Wishes—
Fiction. | New York (N.Y.)—Fiction. | BISAC: JUVENILE
FICTION / Fantasy & Magic. | JUVENILE FICTION / Action &
Adventure / General. | JUVENILE FICTION / Humorous Stories.
Classification: LCC PZ7.1.C765 Ec 2016 | DDC [Fic]—dc23
LC record available at https://lccn.loc.gov/2016006655

Reinforced binding

Visit www.disneybooks.com

SUSTAINABLE   Certified Sourcing
FORESTRY
INITIATIVE   www.sfiprogram.org
               SFI-00993

THIS LABEL APPLIES TO TEXT STOCK

✦

✦

✦

For Henry, who came to Paris for me

Eden's Escape

One

This time, Eden landed on her feet.

When she opened her eyes, she saw that they were planted on black pavement. Black pavement meant a street. She was standing on a street.

Okay, she thought. *But where?* She lifted her eyes.

Directly before her were four yellow taxis, side by side, like the front line of a battalion. To her left and right were buildings so tall, she was as small as a bug in comparison. And in the distance, a narrow slip of bright blue sky framed by more sky-high buildings, as far as she could see.

She'd never been here before; of that, she was certain. And yet, she'd received a genie's education. She'd seen enough photos to know without a doubt where she was.

"New York City," she said softly.

RERRR!!! Car horns rang in her ears.

"Get outta the road!" yelled a man leaning out of a taxi's window. "You tryna get killed?"

The light had changed, and the battalion was ready to charge.

As Eden sprinted to the sidewalk, taxis ripped through the space she left behind. Something heavy bounced on her back, and she felt straps around her shoulders. She was wearing a backpack. Suddenly, it started to vibrate against her back—but there was no time to figure out why right now.

There was no less traffic on the sidewalk, but at least it was made up of mortals on foot rather than cars. The prospect of a collision wasn't nearly as dire.

Mortals. She took a deep breath. She had to stop calling them that.

After all, she was living among them now.

"MOVE!" An old woman in a hot-pink T-shirt shoved her with shocking strength. Eden stumbled sideways into the path of a large family: father, mother, grandparents, and three kids. Each wore a shirt that read I♥NY, and a few of them carried long metal sticks with cell phones attached to the end. They spoke to one another in Russian.

"Should I take her photo?"

"She looks lost."

"I don't think she's American."

"I want a slice of pizza."

"Not now, we're here!"

The members of the family stopped and looked up—so Eden did too. The building in front of them was slim, gray, and dotted with tiny rectangular windows. It rose high into the sky, even higher than all the other buildings. On top was a slender pinnacle that it wore like an elegant crown.

Eden gasped. "The Empire State Building!"

From her left came a warm, rich laugh. "That's right, honey! You know where you're at!" A smiling woman stood at the door, wearing a black captain's hat with a maroon suit jacket and pants. Above her, letters on the building spelled OBSERVATORY ENTRANCE.

"Entrance? That means I can go inside?"

"Course you can, baby!" The woman laughed again. "You can go all the way to the top!"

"To the *top*?" Eden's heart pounded. Imagine looking through a window from the top of this building!

"Sure! Twenty-seven dollars gets you to the eighty-sixth floor."

Eden's hopes fell and shattered like a sheet of glass. After all she'd been through, she *still* didn't have any money.

"Actually, twenty-one dollars if you're twelve or under," the guard amended.

The backpack vibrated against Eden's back again.

"One second," she said, and the guard shrugged amiably. Eden stepped to the side, kneeled to the ground, and removed the backpack.

It was made of brown leather, and larger than the denim one she'd used in San Diego. She unzipped it cautiously, as if something might jump out. At the top, a rolled-up sheet of parchment paper was buzzing insistently. *That* was what had made the backpack vibrate. Eden looked around to see if anyone was paying attention, then unrolled it.

There on the paper was an image of Xavier and Goldie, just as she'd left them. Goldie was rosy-cheeked, with her hair swept neatly into a silver-blond bun; Xavier was handsome and dignified, with dark, slicked-back hair and a pencil-thin mustache.

As Eden watched, the image came to life like a video on a TV screen.

"Hello, Eden," Goldie said fondly. "Welcome to your new adventure."

"You're the first genie ever to live on Earth during her granting career," Xavier said importantly. "You'll live on Earth, but continue granting wishes until you've completed nine hundred and ninety-nine. That is unprecedented. You, my dear, are a pioneer."

"You're going to do *so* well," Goldie assured her. "You're going to thrive!"

"Since you were very young, you've wanted to live

on Earth. You've wanted freedom. And now, you have it," Xavier continued. "But, as you know, with that freedom come greater risks, and greater responsibility."

"*But*, we know that you're ready for those things," Goldie added earnestly. "We believe in you!"

"You begin here, in one of Earth's finest cities," said Xavier. "You'll recognize the building in front of you. Go to the top and take a look around. Your new guardian will meet you there."

"Until we see you again," Goldie said, "good luck out there. We love you."

"And remember, we're always here if you need us."

Xavier waved, and Goldie blew a kiss. Then the message was over.

Eden dug into the backpack. Inside were three pairs of underwear, three pairs of socks, her favorite hunter-green cashmere sweater, a nightgown, a pair of sunglasses, a roll of the enchanted parchment paper, and, at the very top, a wedge of Goldie's carrot cake, wrapped in wax paper. Automatically, Eden pinched off a gooey bite. When it hit her lips, something dizzying and unexpected welled up in her chest, making it hard to swallow. Hastily, she rewrapped the cake and kept looking.

She unzipped the pocket on the front and found a soft brown leather wallet. The billfold held five crisp twenty-dollar bills. Behind the wallet was a slim navy book. PASSPORT, the front read in gold. And, under a seal, UNITED STATES OF AMERICA. She opened it to find, inexplicably, a photo of herself that looked like it was taken yesterday. The passport claimed her birthplace as New York, New York, on a date twelve and a half years earlier. Miraculously, she'd become a U.S. citizen.

Eden had been born a genie in a magic lamp, and had started granting wishes at the age of ten. Since then, she'd granted thirty-six wishes, for twelve mortal wishers. And her masters were the ones who'd made it all possible. Thousands of years ago, they'd enchanted the lamp, created the rules, and designed the granting system.

But in spite of all that, their magical prowess still surprised her once in a while.

She tucked the passport back inside, took out the money, and headed for the top of the Empire State Building.

In the marble-floored entryway, Eden moved toward a metal outline of the building on the back wall. Guards in maroon suits and captain's hats pointed her to a moving set of steel stairs. *My first escalator*, she thought, feeling the cool metal brush her fingertips as she ascended with her hand draped over the black rubber railing.

At the top of the escalator, everyone was corralled into a twisting line with red velvet ropes setting out its course. While she waited, Eden listened to the conversations around her. She heard German, Spanish, and a rare dialect of Cantonese. Besides the guards, it seemed no one here spoke English.

The first room led to a station where people placed their belongings on a conveyor belt, then walked beneath a gray plastic arch.

"What is this?" she asked one of the guards.

"Security." He sounded bored. "Backpack on the belt."

After retrieving her backpack, she boarded an elevator that took her to the eighty-sixth floor. On the elevator ride, the change in air pressure caused a strange sensation in her ears. She yawned to relieve it, and tapped her toes impatiently. But finally the elevator reached the top, and she stepped out and saw the view. And suddenly, the trip was worth all the trouble—and then some.

She darted to the balcony, desperate to eliminate the walls between herself and the unknown. She pressed against the concrete barrier and fitted her face between crisscrossing strips of metal.

Below her, the buildings that made up Manhattan reached expectantly toward the sky. From ground level, they towered mightily; but from up here, they might have been built by children with blocks.

Eden had spent most of her life within the confines of the lamp. She'd grown up with no windows, no light, no vision—only hope for when someone would rub the lamp, allowing her to travel to Earth for a few precious minutes. From the inside, her home had felt palatial, but in reality it was smaller than a shoebox. Similarly, from the sidewalk New York had seemed impossibly big, but now it was an enchanted city in miniature. Up here, she felt like its queen.

She ran around the balcony, taking in the view from each side. She saw Central Park, the Chrysler Building, and One World Trade Center. After studying them for years, she felt like they were pen pals she was finally meeting face-to-face.

On her third lap around, she stopped on the west-facing side to gaze toward the Hudson River. There, a voice came from behind her.

"New York, New York. For me, she can do no wrong. But you caught her on an especially brilliant day."

It was the kind of voice that made you pay attention—the voice of someone *important*. And it spoke perfectly enunciated English.

Eden whipped around to see who it belonged to. The woman was petite—slightly shorter than Eden, in fact. She had creamy white skin, curly chocolate-colored hair, and a grin like a five-year-old on her birthday.

"Pepper!" Eden said with surprise.

She was, of course, a genie alum. She looked exactly like her portrait in the Lamp History course guide. Her career had spanned from 1582 to 1636.

"That's right! Pleased to meet you!" Pepper curtsied, then held a finger playfully to her lips. "But don't blow my cover. At the moment, my name is Quincy."

Eden couldn't fathom what that meant. What she did know was that this must be her guardian. "You're the one who's going to look after me?" she asked.

"Bingo!" Pepper clicked her heels together and beamed.

On paper, Pepper had been one of the friendliest-looking genies. In person, she sparkled like a decked-out Christmas tree.

"Are you a Loyal?" Eden had spotted the thick gold cuff on Pepper's wrist that identified her as a genie. After her last trip to Earth, Eden was wary of all alumni— and petrified of some. She'd had to contend with both the Loyal alumni, who were committed to preserving the lamp's legacy at any cost, and members of Electra, who were determined to seize its power for themselves.

"Technically, yes. But I wasn't part of that mess in San Diego, if that's what you're asking." Pepper wrinkled her freckle-dusted nose. "I don't care for all the politics."

"But you talk to Xavier and Goldie? I've never seen a message from you."

"Not very often—only once a decade or so. I could hardly believe it when they asked for my help! But how could I say no? Guardian for the first genie to ever live on Earth? I never thought I'd see the day!"

Eden blushed. She still wasn't quite sure what to make of it either. Her escape through the lamp's spout and the days she'd spent in San Diego posing as a mortal had convinced Xavier and Goldie of what she'd always suspected: that she wasn't meant to spend the decades to come in the lamp. She really *was* different from the others who'd come before her—so different that the rules had changed for her.

Eden looked down at her own genie bracelet. Unlike Pepper's, hers was active, which meant that even though she was living on Earth now, she was still a genie. When the lamp was rubbed, she'd be summoned to wherever the wisher might be.

But until then, she'd be here, with Pepper. And so far, that seemed like a very good thing. She'd known Pepper for less than five minutes—but already, she couldn't help liking her.

Pepper grabbed her hand. "Come on, let's get out of here! There's so much to see down there."

Two

"The best place to start is smack-dab in the middle of the madness," Pepper declared. So she led them straight up Fifth Avenue.

She was right: New York was a mad, mad city. It pulsed with a million forms of life. A few days ago, when Eden was used to the lamp's silence, San Diego had been a sensory overload. But compared to this, it was as dead as the halls of Mission Beach Middle after the late bell.

The variety of skin tones, hair colors, body types, and clothing styles was endless. Within five blocks, Eden counted twenty-seven breeds of dogs, each tethered to an owner with a leash. One group of six dogs, each a different breed, pulled a single young man who held all of their leashes.

In San Diego, natural beauty was everywhere: the roaring ocean, wide beaches, green hills. But here, there were no trees or plants to speak of, with the exception of the occasional concrete planter with a tentative shrub growing inside. New York was a forest of buildings, not trees.

"New York, New York!" Pepper crowed. "Here, when you're up, you're at the top, and when you're down, you're lower than low. But I promise you this: there's no other place I'd want to be!" Pepper hadn't stopped smiling since Eden had met her. She also moved fast, so Eden had to trot behind her to keep up. She jogged to catch up as they passed the New York Public Library.

"You're lucky," Pepper said. "Sometimes August is so hot, you can't think straight. But today"—holding her arms out wide, she sprang into a graceful leap—"today is *perfect*!" She turned her landing into a pirouette, then continued onward without missing a beat.

Pepper radiated something sort of like magic. When she passed, birds chirped and even the grumpiest people couldn't help smiling. Maybe it was because she didn't really walk; she pranced, throwing in an occasional twirl. And somehow, as she did, she managed to weave deftly through the crowds like she'd been doing it forever. It made Eden wonder. . . .

"How long have you been in New York?"

"Two hundred sixty-six years!" Pepper answered gleefully. "In 1750, I took a ship called the *Patience* from

London. It was smelly and cramped, but seven weeks later, I was here."

"What did the city look like back then?" Eden asked.

"Not much, to be honest. But I fell in love anyway. I knew it was the greatest city in the world. I've always had an eye for potential." Pepper winked. "And ever since then, it keeps getting better." She smiled slyly at Eden. "You know, I should warn you: Manhattan is a darling. If you're not careful, you'll fall for her too."

It was a valid warning. Already, Eden was starting to understand why New York was the setting of countless stories, and the subject of so many songs. Its energy flowed like adrenaline through her veins. There was a desperate, thrilling sense of motion in the air.

"I know this city inside out. I'm the best tour guide there is!" Pepper beamed. "So tell me, what would you like to see?"

"This." Eden watched an old man tooting an out-of-tune trumpet on the sidewalk. *"Life."*

"Right, then. In New York, you won't run out of that!" Pepper took Eden's hand in hers and swung it. "Look!" She pointed up at a bronze statue that Eden recognized: Atlas, holding the heavens aloft in his muscular arms. It stood in front of Rockefeller Center. Eden walked in a slow circle around it, staring up into the clouds through Atlas's globe.

"How did someone *make* this?" she asked in awe.

"Pretty incredible, right?" Pepper agreed. "Sometimes we don't give mortals enough credit."

As they continued up Fifth Avenue, Pepper rattled off facts and funny stories about the places they passed.

"That way is MoMA, the Museum of Modern Art. One time, eleven years ago, I was part of a performance-art piece there. I had to sing and act out 'I'm a Little Teapot' for hours on end!"

Then: "There's Bergdorf Goodman, the best place to play dress-up!"

And then: "That's the Plaza Hotel. In 1954 I lived there for a month, and had breakfast in bed every morning. It was *heaven*!"

Eden smiled. Pepper seemed to have a rich personal history with every single block.

"And here," Pepper said triumphantly, "is Central Park!"

The lawn spread out before them, covered with mortals enjoying the dreamy day. It was a giant green oasis in the concrete city. To Eden, it was like a welcome breeze through an open window.

"This is the *best* place in Manhattan to walk, run, read, and, in the winter, ice-skate! But do you want to know my favorite thing to do here in the summer?" Pepper took both of Eden's hands in hers as they reached an open patch.

"What?" Eden giggled.

"Dance!" Pepper spun her around in circles until they were both so dizzy, they couldn't walk straight. Pepper crashed head-on into a studious-looking young man who looked at her like she was insane.

Eden couldn't stop laughing. Maybe Pepper *was* insane—but in the best kind of way. Even though she was over four hundred years old, she acted like a kid on a playground. Eden had a feeling you could never get bored with her.

"Fancy an ice cream?" Pepper asked once she could walk straight again.

They bought cones of soft-serve from a stand, then found a clear spot and sat down in the grass.

Even after the days she'd just spent in the California summer, sunlight was still harsh to Eden's sensitive eyes. She put on the sunglasses from her backpack and surveyed the mortals lounging around them.

One woman was facing away from her, sitting cross-legged and alone. The way her honey-colored hair cascaded down her back made Eden's temperature rise ten degrees.

"What's wrong?" Pepper asked, looking up from her ice cream.

"Is that—" Eden gasped. But at that moment, the woman turned and smiled at an approaching friend. She had the face of a teenager, fresh and soft-featured, without the sharply defined jaw and cheekbones Eden had been dreading. She let out the breath she'd been holding.

"Electra really got into your head, didn't they?" Pepper was watching her curiously. She made a *tsk* sound. "What a shame."

Now Eden was embarrassed. "I know I don't need to worry anymore," she said. "I don't have the lamp, or even a way of knowing where it is. They have no use for me now, right?"

"You'd think," Pepper agreed.

"Do the Loyals know I'm here?"

"Don't think so. Xavier and Goldie said I'm the only one they told." Pepper popped the pointy end of her ice cream cone in her mouth. "So let's keep it that way, shall we?"

Three

After a full day of exploring the city, they headed for Pepper's apartment.

Pepper explained that she lived on 44th Street, between Seventh and Eighth Avenues. That didn't mean much to Eden. But her ears perked up when Pepper said they were going to be passing through Times Square.

Though Eden had seen photos of the world-famous intersection, they couldn't do justice to the experience of being there in person. Light and color assailed you from every direction. Advertising covered the massive buildings. Some of them were plastered with larger-than-life movie posters; others had huge TV screens playing videos. There were tickers with headlines running eagerly across, and billboards promoting Broadway shows. And people *everywhere*. Like at the Empire State Building, there were people from all over the world, speaking dozens of languages. There were people in uniforms recruiting attendees for comedy clubs and bus tours, and even people dressed up like cartoon characters and superheroes, strolling around and posing for photos.

Eden was so dazzled that she had to stand still and soak it all in for a few minutes. Pepper waited patiently, answering all her questions. When she was finally ready to move on, they stopped by Pepper's favorite pizza place and picked up a pie to bring back to her apartment building. They carried it six floors up a dark, narrow staircase to the roof so they could enjoy Manhattan's signature food and its lit-up skyline at the same time. Then they settled in next to each other, cross-legged, with the pizza box in front of them and the night sky above them.

Eden bit into her first slice eagerly, but immediately opened her mouth in surprise and waved her hand in front of it.

"Oh no!" Pepper said. "The cheese is hot! I should have warned you!"

"Too late!" Eden swallowed and grinned. "Oh well. It's worth it."

"That's my girl." Pepper took another bite and winced. "Ouch! See, it's so good, I keep eating it anyway!"

Eden threw her head back and laughed. She couldn't imagine being happier.

The night was so warm that she was still comfortable

in the tank top and shorts she'd been wearing since San Diego. Suddenly she realized she hadn't slept since then. She'd gone from the amusement park showdown with the alumni, to her conversation with Xavier and Goldie in the lamp, to the middle of Fifth Avenue. Between changing time zones and the lamp's time-bending capabilities, she didn't even know how long it had been.

But she still wasn't tired. The city's energy had her buzzing. She wondered if she'd ever need sleep again.

"I used to work at this pizza place," Pepper said as she took another slice. "I wish I still did. The food at the diner where I've been working for the past few months is *awful*. But tomorrow's my last day! Xavier and Goldie told me to quit, so I'll have all the time in the world to show you around."

"Hold on. You work?" Eden couldn't imagine it.

"Of course! I may be immortal, but I've got to pay bills!"

It was a good point, Eden supposed.

"I've worked at hundreds of places all over the city: restaurants, bars, cafés, boutiques, department stores, jewelry stores, barbershops, cupcake shops..."

"Do you like those jobs?"

"Well, there's good to be found in anything," Pepper said. "Friends to be made, things to be learned. But the jobs themselves?" She wrinkled her nose. "No, I wouldn't say I like them."

"So why not get a job you like?"

"I do have a job I like—just not at the moment. But it won't be long now. Almost fifty years have passed." She flushed with pleasure.

Now Eden was really confused. "Does this have something to do with how you said to call you Quincy?"

A sneaky smile spread across Pepper's face. "You're a smart kid, you know that?"

Grinning, Eden took another slice of pizza and got comfortable. She had a feeling there was a good story coming.

"Each of us is born with a specific destiny. For me, that destiny was, of course, to be a genie; but after that, to become an actress."

Things started to click into place. Pepper's melodious voice. Her contagious exuberance. The way she weaved and danced through crowds of people.

The closest Eden had come to the theater was hearing Xavier belt show tunes in the morning. But from what she'd learned, Pepper being a performer made perfect sense.

"How did you know it was ... your destiny?"

Pepper hushed her voice and looked around to ensure they were alone on the roof. "I learned it on my very first granting. My first wisher was William Shakespeare."

"That's right!" Eden remembered. "I read about that

in the course guide! There was a question about it on a quiz."

"What was the answer?"

"I think it was 1592."

"Correct," Pepper said with a smile. "Each of his wishes," she recalled dreamily, "was for his career. And he wished *brilliantly*. Well, from the way things turned out, that's obvious. But honestly, I don't think any other mortal, dead or alive, could wish like that man."

Even though Eden knew essentially what had happened, Pepper brought the story to life. Her wonderful voice was so enthralling, Eden would have listened to her read the dictionary.

"He took his time, pondering his wishes, and we started to talk. He was thoughtful and careful—not manic, like most of them. You know what I mean. And *kind*. Even though I was ten years old, just a child, he gave me *respect*." Pepper lay back on the roof's rough surface and rested her head on her folded hands. Eden did the same. With all the lights of the city, you couldn't see many stars, which was disappointing. Back in the lamp, she'd dreamed of picking out constellations in the sky. But in a way, this was better. Whereas stars were eternal and immovable, electricity was evidence of real, present, fallible mortal life. And wasn't that what she'd come here for?

"He showed me the play he was writing: *A Midsummer Night's Dream*. There were kinks to iron out with the verse, and he wanted to hear it read aloud. So I did it, changing voices for the parts. I *acted* for him. He was my first audience. And he loved it." There was pride in her voice. "He even asked me for suggestions. Helena's line 'Though she be but little, she is fierce'—that was mine. He told me that someday I'd make a fine actor." She turned toward Eden, propping her head up on one hand. "So I listened."

"Who wouldn't?" Eden rested her own head on a hand too. Shakespeare was one of a select few mortals she genuinely admired.

"When I finished my nine hundred ninety-nine wishes, I wished to live on Earth forever and perform onstage for generations. I wished that they'd love me the way William loved me."

Eden was touched that Pepper had confided her thousandth wish so freely. In the lamp, Xavier and Goldie guarded the genies' thousandth wishes like precious secrets.

Pepper blinked. She lay flat on her back again and murmured, as if to reproach her younger self: "If I'd only known then what I know now."

"What do you mean?" Eden asked. "That sounds like a good wish to me."

There was a sign across the street with a flashing light that illuminated Pepper's face. The light blinked pink, then purple, then blue. Pink, purple, blue.

"Well, there were challenges right off the bat. I started out in London, where I'd first met William. I couldn't wait to see him again. It was only after I got there that I found out . . . he was dead." The colored light played on her face: pink, purple, blue. "That was when I realized, even if we're immortal, death can still hurt us."

Something sharp twinged in Eden's heart, like a guitar string snapping.

"Once I'd mourned him, I decided the next best thing would be to honor his memory. I could act in his plays. But then I found out I wasn't allowed to."

"Because you were a woman."

"Right. It was 1636. The English thought having a woman onstage would be scandalous. Men played all the women's parts. And I have to admit, some of them did a fine job. Once, during a production of *Romeo and Juliet*, I absolutely *sobbed* when Juliet leaned over her balcony and professed her love to Romeo. I'd completely forgotten Juliet was a boy with a wig! *There's* a testament to the power of theater." Pepper nodded, seeming to agree with herself. "Women were acting in other parts of Europe, but I wanted to be in London." A smile played on the corners of her mouth, and she sat up again. "So I changed the rules."

"How?"

"In 1660, I was the first woman to act onstage in England. I was Margaret Hughes, playing Desdemona in *Othello*. What a night that was!" For a moment, Pepper seemed to have drifted right back there.

"Margaret Hughes?" Eden prompted.

"That was the name I used for those first twenty years—my first career. In a job where people see you onstage every night, that's about the longest you can get away with before they start talking about why you never age." She rubbed her nose.

Eden had never thought much about the logistics of immortality on Earth. Perhaps, like most things, it wasn't as simple as it seemed.

"So what then?"

"Then I changed my name to Emily Bankman. I moved between tiny towns in England, working as a governess and cleaning houses. When I could save up enough for it, I'd put on a big hat and a scarf to hide my face, and steal away to London to see a show." She clasped a hand over her chest. "It broke my heart to be away from the theater. But I knew that eventually my time would come again."

"And did it?"

"Fifty years later. I moved back to London as Emily, and did it all over again."

"Didn't people remember you?"

"No. I'd been away for fifty years, remember. I generally do fifteen to twenty years of work, then fifty years waiting to work again. The way I see it, I have to keep a cycle of approximately seventy years—a pretty average life span for a mortal. Mortals rarely pay attention to their parents' icons. If I happen to look like another generation's star, no one's the wiser."

"And that works?"

"So far, so good." Pepper shrugged. She picked a piece of pepperoni off a pizza slice. "Of course, nowadays it's tougher, with the Internet. I've got to be more careful this time around."

"So after Emily Bankman..."

"After eighteen years performing as Emily, I became Rosalie Handelman and boarded the *Patience*. When I arrived in New York, I didn't know a soul; I realized I could start afresh. So I started Rosalie's career immediately. It was a risk, with so many people coming from London. I had to wriggle my way out of a few sticky situations. But it all turned out right. And those were beautiful years. Broadway was just getting its legs. It was the only time I got to work for so many years straight. Pure bliss. After that, I knew I'd be a lifer in New York."

"I want to see you perform!" Eden said.

"Well, God willing, it won't be long. Next month, fifty years will have passed. Very soon, I'll start auditioning—with my new name, Quincy Abbott."

"Quincy!"

"It all comes together now, doesn't it?"

It was a crazy story—but what wasn't, these days? Best of all, it showed that Pepper was different from the other alumni. Immortality hadn't made her bitter and jaded, like the Loyals at the pool at Mission Beach Middle. She didn't spend her centuries in mad pursuit of vengeance, like the alumni members of Electra. She spent as much of her life as possible living out her dream in her favorite city. She loved the world, and she loved her place in it. To Eden, that seemed like a good way to live.

"After Rosalie, I had three more careers. By the most recent one, musical theater was in full swing. I got to sing *and* act *and* dance! It was a dream come true."

"Xavier loves musicals," Eden said.

Pepper's eyes grew wide, and she squeezed Eden's forearm. "You've got to be kidding me."

"I'm serious! He used to sing a show tune every morning to wake me up."

Pepper laughed like crazy. "I never would have guessed it!" She wiped an eye. "What was your favorite?"

"I always liked 'On the Street Where You Live.'"

"From *My Fair Lady*! Divine! I played Eliza Doolittle from 1957 to '59."

Now that Eden thought about it, Xavier must have learned about musicals like he learned about everything else on Earth: through trips made when he climbed out of the lamp's spout. Although operas had existed for centuries, modern-day musicals weren't performed until the twentieth century. The morning songs couldn't have been going on for long.

How many evenings might he have spent in Broadway theaters, maybe even on this very street? He would have bought his ticket quietly and sat in the mezzanine, or one of the back rows, enjoying the show among mortals who would never have suspected he was collecting information to bring back to an enchanted lamp.

Could Xavier have watched Pepper perform in one of those shows? It was certainly possible. Maybe he knew more about the alumni than he let on, even to them.

"Speaking of Xavier," Pepper said, "we should send them a message to let them know we've found each other. Did they give you some parchment?"

Eden opened the backpack she'd arrived with and pulled out the roll of parchment paper. Pepper expertly tore off a section and held it in front of them so it could record their message.

"Here we are!" she said sunnily. "Bright lights, big city! We found each other just like you planned, and we've been exploring together ever since."

"Hi! Thanks for the backpack!" Eden added, waving.

"Hey, what's that?" Pepper asked, noticing the wrapped-up carrot cake in the backpack. Eden pulled it out and unwrapped it. Pepper tore off half the piece, then tapped it against Eden's. "Cheers!" They both took a bite. Pepper's eyes rolled back in bliss. "Heaven! You've still got it, Goldie!" She wiped frosting off her lips. "Anyway, if you need us, you know where to find us!" Pepper and Eden blew a kiss toward the parchment paper; then Pepper rolled it up, gave it a squeeze, and off it went to its magical destination.

"Now," Pepper said, taking another bite of carrot cake, "I want to hear more about you! Tell me about San Diego. Not the bad things—let's not think about them. Only the wonderful parts."

There was a pang in Eden's heart. Despite what had happened with Electra and the Loyals, parts of her trip to San Diego *had* been wonderful. All day, thoughts of Tyler and Sasha had tugged at the back of her mind. So she told Pepper all about them: how Tyler would surf all day if he could; how Sasha was fiercely competitive, and even more fiercely loyal. The way they cared for each other and their dad. The way they'd tried to keep her on Earth.

"I'm so glad!" Pepper burst out. "Friends make everything better, don't they?"

Eden smiled and nodded, remembering. Suddenly, something occurred to her. She reached into the back pocket of her shorts and felt a stiff piece of paper. She pulled it out and laughed. It was the photo of her and Tyler on the roller coaster. It had traveled from San

Diego to the lamp with her, and now it had made the trip back to Earth with her too.

In the picture, their hands were raised high in the air and their faces showed pure elation. Pepper gasped when she saw it. "How *wonderful*!" she exclaimed. "You look so *happy*!"

"I was," Eden agreed.

"When do you think you'll see them again?"

All of a sudden, Eden was nervous. "I don't know. I mean, how would I? They live on the other side of the country."

Pepper laughed. "You're a genie who just changed the ancient rules of her lamp! How could the width of one little country stop you?"

Eden's cheeks flushed. Pepper had a point.

"Let's take a trip to the West Coast!"

"Wouldn't that be expensive?"

"Don't worry about that!" Pepper said. "I told you, Xavier and Goldie want me to quit my job so I can look after you full-time. They're going to make sure we have enough money."

"How?"

"They set up a fund at the bank. Every week, money will be automatically transferred into my account. It'll be more than enough for us to live on. And more than enough for an occasional trip to California." She winked. "Come on. It'll be so much fun!"

"I don't know their phone numbers," Eden protested. "Or their address."

"But you know their last name, and the city they live in."

"What good does that do?"

"Hello! Remember what we were just talking about? The Internet?"

Eden shrugged. Xavier regarded the Internet with disdain, and had covered it only briefly in the lamp, so Eden knew very little about it. Perhaps it *could* provide a way to get in touch with the Rockwells.

If she was honest, the bigger problem was that she was afraid. She'd caused so much trouble in their lives. Because of her, their father had been taken hostage by Electra. Because of her, they'd nearly lost the only parent they had left.

What kind of a friend did things like that?

Pepper pulled out her phone. "What are their names?"

They searched Tyler's name first. There were results for a character in *Teenage Mutant Ninja Turtles*, an electrician in St. Louis, a professor at the University of Wisconsin, and a boy who'd won a spelling bee in Baltimore. "Nope, none of these is him." Eden tried not to sound relieved.

"That's okay—I've just got to add that he's in San

Diego." Pepper typed in something else and touched one of the search results. "Here he is!"

When Eden saw the screen, her heart leapt into her throat.

It was *him*.

Tan skin with freckles, shiny straight chestnut-brown hair. A wide smile that showed his slightly crooked teeth.

Seeing his face made Eden feel a little dizzy.

"It *is* him, isn't it?" Pepper grinned. Eden swallowed and nodded.

The photo was on a profile page about him. It listed his name, his school, and where he lived. Pepper scrolled down to show more photos. One of him laughing by his locker at school. One of him and Devin, hoisting their surfboards over their heads. One with his arm hooked around Sasha's neck.

"That's Sasha," Eden said.

Pepper tapped the screen, and there was a profile page for her, too. In the main photo, she wore her volleyball uniform and stood in front of a net with a ball tucked under her arm.

"Let's send them a message!" Pepper said. "Do you want to set up a profile?"

"I probably shouldn't," Eden said quickly. "What if the Electric see it?"

"Good point. We'll message them from mine."

"Maybe," Eden said uncertainly. "Can I think about it first?"

Pepper's eyebrows lifted quizzically. "Sure you can." She stretched her arms and yawned. "Look, kid, it's been a gorgeous day, but I'm exhausted. What do you say we get some sleep?"

Her apartment was on the building's top floor. It was tiny—a studio, Pepper called it. That meant that a single room served as the living room, bedroom, and kitchen. A big bed hid most of the dull wood that covered the floor. In the "kitchen" was a refrigerator that was shorter than Eden, a sink, and about a square foot of counter space that an old coffeemaker barely fit on. The only other piece of furniture was a stool with a black cushioned seat, pulled up to a large window.

The window redeemed the whole apartment. Through it was a direct view of an old Broadway theater where a large sign said MATILDA was currently playing. You could also see other theaters with titles of different shows, all the way down the block. A show must have just ended, because theatergoers streamed down the street, many of them arm in arm. Eden had a feeling that when Pepper was home, she was usually sitting on that stool.

"It's not much," Pepper said when they walked in. Suddenly, she seemed insecure. "After the lamp—"

"It's perfect," Eden said.

"Really?" Pepper's eyes were hopeful. It was hard to believe an ages-old alum who'd performed onstage for millions of people could be affected by Eden's opinion, but clearly she was.

"Really. Look at this view! It's almost like you're at the theater."

"That's my favorite part." Pepper seemed grateful that Eden understood. "I'd live in a closet if it meant I was on Broadway."

They took turns washing up in the sliver of a bathroom, then lay together under a thin cotton sheet in Pepper's bed. It was sort of like when Goldie used to come to Eden's room in the lamp for girls' sleepovers, except that this time, sound and light from the restless city bled through the curtain. It seemed Manhattan wouldn't let you forget that even when you slept, it raged on—and there was nothing you could do about it.

All at once, fatigue hit Eden like a sinking, falling feeling.

"Good night," said Pepper softly.

"Good night, Pepper." Even as she said it, Eden was drifting away, here in this slip of an apartment hovering above New York City, to one of the sweetest sleeps of her life.

Four

Over the next two weeks, Pepper educated Eden in the magic of New York.

Technically—well, legally, at least—Eden should have been in school. Just like in San Diego, schools in New York had resumed following summer break this week. But neither Eden nor Pepper was in a rush to get her there. "I'm your private tutor," Pepper justified. "Pepper's school of street smarts. It's more useful than anything they'd teach you. You already know it all anyway."

It was a good point. Very quickly it had become clear that despite the days she'd spent in San Diego, Eden didn't know much about living on Earth. Pepper insisted that was completely normal. There was a sharp learning curve for every genie when she retired. Life on Earth was a far cry from the insulated, isolated life inside the lamp. And although Xavier's schooling had provided more than enough knowledge about earthly things, a lot of it hadn't proven very practical. Being able to determine the weather pattern that caused a rainstorm didn't do much good if you didn't know where to buy an umbrella—or, once you had one, how to open it.

But Pepper was an excellent teacher: patient, understanding, and always entertaining. Her lessons took place as they covered the city, laughing and exploring. They picked up bagels for breakfast, dodged street vendors on Canal Street, eyed tigers in the Central Park Zoo, skipped across the Brooklyn Bridge, ate spaghetti in Little Italy, discussed art at the Met, and cheered and jeered at a Yankees game.

One day, while they window-shopped in SoHo, Pepper explained how she'd come to live where she did.

"Lots of New Yorkers turn up their noses at my neighborhood," she said. "They say Times Square is too hectic, and the Theater District is packed with tourists." She shrugged. "I felt that way too, for a while. I've lived in nooks and crannies all over the city, from the Financial District to Harlem. Even Brooklyn for a year." She wrinkled her nose. "Never again," she whispered, then giggled. "But the Theater District called me back. For me, it's the heart of the city. It's everything I love most about Manhattan. Plus, I like having people around me. Being immortal has its perks, but it can also be lonely. You can't get close to many people. It's hard to have friends."

"But you *do* have friends," Eden said. "A lot of them."

She'd noticed that the couple in the apartment across the hall, neighbors washing their clothes at the Laundromat, and even people begging for money on the street lit up when they saw her. "Quincy!" they'd say, like they'd been waiting for her all day. Somehow she remembered all their names, and asked about their children, their dogs, or their sick great-aunts.

"Well, there are a lot of people in this city!" Pepper said. "Hey, guess what! I've got a surprise for you."

"What is it?"

Smiling slyly, Pepper slipped two rectangular pieces of paper from her wallet and handed them to Eden.

"Tickets?"

"Broadway tickets," she said grandly. "For tomorrow night."

"Pepper!" Eden looked at them closely. "For *My Fair Lady*!"

"You're going to love it!" Pepper did a happy little spin on the sidewalk.

Eden was giddy with joy. "I don't know what to say," she said. "Except, thank you."

"Don't be silly." Pepper grinned. "It's for me, too! I get to go see a show with my friend!"

And that was, Eden realized, what they'd become. Pepper wasn't just a guardian; she was her friend.

That evening, Eden wore a light-pink-and-white-striped sundress Pepper had bought for her. Its thin straps crossed between her shoulders; the bodice was fitted but not too tight, and the loose skirt was exactly the right length. Eden liked it better than any other dress she'd ever owned.

Instead of braiding her long blond hair like usual, she pulled it into a high ponytail. Pepper had been vigilant about making sure her lamp-protected skin was covered with sunscreen, but she was pretty sure she'd tanned at least a fraction of a shade. Examining herself in Pepper's cloudy bathroom mirror, Eden decided she looked like a normal, happy mortal. And she had to marvel at that. A few weeks ago, who'd have guessed she'd be here?

"Ready?" Pepper had taken a curling iron to her hair, making her normally unruly curls full and defined. In her Grecian-style white dress, she looked like a grown-up cherub.

"I don't have any pockets to put my cell phone in."

"Put it in my purse," said Pepper, holding it open. "You won't need it anyway. You'll be with me."

They were meeting Pepper's friends in the East Village for something called karaoke. Eden wasn't sure what karaoke was, but with Pepper, it was bound to be fun.

They took the subway downtown, then walked past redbrick buildings with ground-floor tattoo shops and delis. Finally they arrived at one with a sign that read TRA LA LA KARAOKE in bold green letters on a yellow field.

The entrance led into a darkened, dingy sort of room. On the left, a tattooed girl stood behind a bar. Throughout the room, people huddled around scuffed black tables, laughing and drinking. On the walls were faded posters of what seemed to be album covers. Squinting through the semi-dark, Eden read the names on them: Prince, Boyz II Men, Mariah Carey.

In the back of the room was a small stage raised a step above the floor. Behind it was a TV screen that displayed song lyrics in blue, superimposed over a romantic scene on a beach.

On the stage, a heavyset man was crooning a horribly out-of-tune love song into a microphone.

Eden clapped a hand over her mouth to hold back a giggle. She glanced at Pepper and saw that she was doing the exact same thing.

"Quincy!" called a voice. A dark-haired man and woman were waving from one of the tables.

But the security guard posted inside the door held out a thick arm to stop them. "No kids in here," he grunted.

Pepper shot him her sweetest smile. "What's your name?"

Within a minute, she'd changed his mind.

Her friends at the table were Eduardo and Felicia, a married couple from Argentina. Two skinny, bearded guys named Oliver and Sebastian soon joined them too. The six of them discussed politics, the economy, and the Matisse exhibit Eden and Pepper had just seen at the Met. The adults sipped beers while Eden drank a Shirley Temple. But even though she was decades (or, in Pepper's case, centuries) younger than the others, they didn't treat her like a kid. They made her feel like she belonged.

As they talked, various people took the stage and sang. Some of them didn't sound bad, but others were downright awful. Either way, it was entertaining.

When a woman onstage began wailing a horribly off-key country ballad, Oliver smiled at Pepper. "Isn't it about time you got up there?" Eden noticed that his teeth were slightly crooked, just like Tyler's.

"You first," Pepper said with a wink.

"You've heard her sing, right?" Felicia asked Eden, leaning toward her. She closed her eyes and clutched her heart. "I have never heard anything so beautiful in my life!"

"Actually, no," Eden realized. Considering all Pepper's success through the years, Eden had to assume she had talent—but she'd never seen or heard it for herself.

"Seriously?" Oliver said. "Wait till you hear this. She's unbelievable."

"You two first," Pepper insisted. "While I get us another round."

Oliver and Sebastian performed a song called "Ice Ice Baby," including a few choreographed dance moves. They got the whole room laughing and singing along. Pepper laughed so hard, she nearly fell off her chair. Then the woman from before got up for yet another out-of-tune country ballad. But finally, it was Pepper's turn.

Even as she took the stage, something in the atmosphere changed. Conversations came to a halt, and every eye turned toward her.

It wasn't just that she looked pretty, though she was a vision in her white dress. There was something else about Pepper. It was the same quality people responded to on the street when she passed, and the reason she collected friends the way sun-ripened fruit collects bees.

That special presence of hers. That irresistible, radiant joy.

Maybe it was that mysterious thing Marilyn Monroe had wished for from Faye in 1945: *star quality.*

As the opening notes played, Pepper closed her eyes and swayed. There was a dreamy smile on her face. She looked happier—and, somehow, more like herself—than Eden had ever seen her before.

She raised the mike to her mouth and started to sing.

"I have often walked down this street before
But the pavement always stayed beneath my feet before
All at once am I several stories high
Knowing I'm on the street where you live..."

Eden's heart pounded. Unbelievably, she knew this one.

Of all the songs in the world, Pepper had chosen one for her.

And she was incredible. She cast a spell on the room. A quick glance around confirmed that she'd mesmerized every last person. Eden suspected they felt the way she did: desperate to soak in every second. Nothing could make her look away.

"Oh! The towering feeling
Just to know somehow you are near.
The overpowering feeling
That any second you may suddenly appear!"

With Pepper onstage, the dingy karaoke bar was suddenly glamorous. No longer was Tra La La a hole-in-the-wall with happy-hour specials and dirty floors. Pepper made it the stuff of legends.

Eden was keenly aware that this—the room of fifty people, most of whom didn't know each other, sharing in the marvel of this performance; the voice that came from the lungs of her guardian, breathing and singing and swaying onstage—this was *life*! Life had never been sweeter or truer than in this moment.

She didn't want the moment to end.

"People stop and stare, they don't bother me
For there's nowhere else on Earth that I would rather be,"
Pepper belted.

By now the whole bar was clapping and cheering. Some audience members had gotten to their feet.

"Let the time go by, I won't care if I
Can be here on the street where you live!"

"What did I tell you?" Oliver whispered.

Eden shook her head, speechless. She couldn't stop smiling. Pepper locked eyes with her and grinned back. She extended an arm and pointed straight at her.

"People stop and stare, they don't bother me
For there's nowhere else on Earth that I would rather be
Let the time go by, I won't care if I
Can be here on the street where you live!"

Happiness pulsed through Eden's veins. She felt like the luckiest girl in the world.

The song ended in an uproar of applause, whistles, cheers, and shouts of "Bravo!" Laughing, Pepper curtsied and hurried off the stage.

"Pepper!" Eden said as Pepper reached the table. "You were amazing!"

"Do you really think so?" Out of the spotlight, she was still the same old Pepper. And just like in the apartment, she actually cared what Eden thought.

"Are you kidding? That was the best thing I've ever heard!"

Pepper hugged her tight. "It was all for you, kid."

She settled back into her chair, and three men appeared, each from a different part of the room. Each of them looked desperate to meet her.

As the first man introduced himself, Eden felt a strange shudder through her body. There was a sense of acceleration in her chest—a distinct feeling that she knew well.

It was a good thing all eyes were on Pepper, because that meant no one was watching when Eden disappeared.

Five

"Well, I'll be!"

Eden was face-to-face with her new wisher. He was clutching the lamp in hands that were covered by latex gloves. He looked younger than forty, but older than thirty. His thick dark-blond hair was parted on one side. He was small in stature, short and slight, wearing blue jeans and a faded red sweatshirt emblazoned with the word STANFORD. But he wore big, round-lensed eyeglasses, and his mouth was full of big white teeth.

"It's true!" he marveled. He spoke English with an American accent. In fact, it was a variety of American accent that Eden hadn't heard much of. He spoke more slowly and stretched his vowels out longer than most people in New York. In the lamp, she'd learned about common linguistic patterns in different regions. She was pretty sure that this was the way people spoke in the southeastern United States.

Eden looked around. They were in a windowless white box of a room. Long fluorescent lights striped the smooth white ceiling and bathed the space in a harsh, unnatural glow. It was profoundly different from the crowded karaoke bar she'd been whisked away from.

A woman and two men flanked the wisher. Both men wore white lab coats. One was tall and blond. There was a stethoscope around his neck, and a surgical mask over his mouth. The other man was small and dark-skinned. Like the wisher, he was wearing latex gloves.

The woman was tanned and petite, with a tough square jaw and brown hair pulled into a low ponytail. She wore a white blouse and olive-colored slacks.

"Jean Luc." The wisher handed the lamp to the smaller man. "As we discussed."

Jean Luc nodded and strode away, exiting the room through its only door.

An uneasy feeling shot through Eden. "Where's he going with that?"

But the wisher didn't answer—just stared at her in fascination. "Patrick."

The man with the stethoscope approached her. "Sit here," he said gruffly. He sounded American too, though he lacked the wisher's Southern drawl.

Alarmed, Eden took a step back. The Achilles tendon just above her heel hit something hard and sharp.

She whipped around. Behind her was a tan leather

chair with a headrest, thick cushions, wide armrests, and the footrest that she'd kicked. It wasn't a regular living-room armchair; there was something more clinical about it.

"Go on, take a seat," the wisher urged.

The tall blond man took her elbow and tried to guide her into the chair.

"Hey!" Eden yanked her arm away. The man hopped back, hands held in front of him so she could see them.

"Careful, Patrick," said the wisher. He was staring at Eden as if she were a rare wild animal he'd never seen up close.

He placed a hand on his chest. "My name is David Brightly." He gestured toward the other man. "This is Doctor Patrick Evans." Dr. Evans looked like he thought Eden might bite him. "And this is Jane Johnston." He indicated the woman, who stared at her without blinking.

"Patrick wants to check your vitals. Heartbeat, blood pressure. Won't hurt ya. Is that all right?"

"Why?"

The wisher didn't answer—just stared through his big round glasses.

"Where am I?" Eden asked.

"In a research facility that belongs to Brightly Tech."

"What's that?" The name sounded vaguely familiar, but she wasn't sure why.

"My company." He beamed, showing his big white teeth. A slight overbite made them even more prominent, and made Eden think of a horse's mouth. "Accordin' to *Forbes*, we're the biggest technology company in the world. And accordin' to most folks you meet, the best."

A warning bell buzzed in Eden's head. Since Xavier had never covered technology as a part of her education back in the lamp, it was mostly a mystery to her. She could barely even operate her cell phone—which, she suddenly realized, she'd left in Pepper's purse.

Eden thought back to Tra La La Karaoke. By now Pepper would have realized she'd been summoned for a granting, but Felicia, Eduardo, and her other friends would be wondering where she'd disappeared to. Eden winced, imagining Pepper having to invent excuses for her.

"Let's make this quick," she said to Brightly. "You've got three wishes. Ready, go."

Brightly cocked his head.

"Hello! Didn't you hear me? I'm going to grant three wishes for you!"

"You need to calm down, little lady." Brightly was still looking at her like she was something he'd read about in an encyclopedia.

His lack of interest in the wishes was puzzling. Normally mortals were so ecstatic, they couldn't spit out their fantasies fast enough. She'd never seen a reaction like this.

"I'm a genie," she said, in case he'd somehow missed that part. "You rubbed my lamp. I'm here to grant your wishes. So let's get going!"

Brightly turned to the woman. "Jane. Could you be so kind as to help Dr. Evans?"

"Help him with what?" Eden's heart started beating faster.

The two men locked eyes. Brightly gave Patrick a slight nod.

"*Hello!* Help him with *what*?" Eden repeated. "You'd better tell me this instant!"

Jane Johnston darted at her. She and Patrick seized Eden's arms and pushed her toward the seat.

When Eden was still at least a foot away, she felt a force coming from the chair, pulling her into it. It was like the magnets she'd learned about in the lamp's lesson room.

The magnetic force was far stronger than she was; there was no way to resist it. Within moments, she was in the chair.

Her back was pinned to its back, her thighs were glued to its seat, and her limbs were stuck to its arm- and footrests. Desperately she tried to pull away, but she couldn't lift a finger.

As she screamed senselessly for help, Eden couldn't help thinking that this had to be her worst granting yet.

For the next few hours, they poked, prodded, and examined her. Dr. Patrick Evans listened to her heartbeat, took her temperature, and measured her blood pressure. He reclined the chair, looked inside her ears and nose and down her throat, and shone a light in her eyes.

He tried to draw blood from the crook inside her elbow, but his needle wouldn't puncture her skin.

"Well, I'll *be*!" Brightly exclaimed as he watched in wonder. Jane took notes on an electronic tablet, and even recorded a close-up video.

Of course, Eden knew why they couldn't draw blood: because her genie bracelet was active. That meant she was under the lamp's protection, and, therefore, immortal. Nothing they could do would inflict harm on her body.

That didn't mean it didn't hurt, though. She felt every one of the fifteen attempts.

"Subject seems to be immune to bodily harm, but does appear to experience pain." Brightly pushed up his glasses. "Jane, make a note of that."

They did manage to get clippings from her fingernails and cut a lock of hair from her ponytail. Eden watched as Patrick sealed the hard white half-moons in one tiny plastic bag, and the white-blond hair in another.

After a while, she stopped screaming. She was exhausted, and anyway, once they got the results they wanted, she had to assume Brightly would finally make his wishes.

It was strange. Before now, she'd desperately wanted every granting to last and last. Now that she wanted to get this one over with, it felt like it would never end.

"Are you done yet?" she asked when they seemed to be slowing down.

"Nah," Brightly said, watching as Jane input more notes. "But we're movin' on to the next portion of testing." He beamed that big, horsey smile. "You're an interesting specimen."

Her heart sank. If she had the lamp, she could make a request for reentry, which allowed a genie to escape in the event of a granting gone wrong. Before, it would have sent her back inside the lamp. But now that her home was with Pepper, it would take her back to New York, right by her side.

Unfortunately, without the lamp, there was no way to make the request. She'd have to wait until three wishes had been granted.

Until a few weeks ago, when the rules had changed, her genie bracelet wouldn't have allowed the lamp to be taken away from her. But now, since she'd come to live on Earth, the connection between her and the lamp had changed. They might have taken it anywhere.

"If you don't bring me the lamp right now, you're going to lose your wishes!" Eden said. Threatening wishers with the prospect of losing their wishes had always been effective in the past.

But Brightly was different. He grinned at her, looking amused. "You're a tough little cookie, aren't ya?"

At least they hadn't touched or mentioned the bracelet. As long as it was on her wrist, she was safe—and so was the lamp, wherever it might be.

"What's up with this chair, anyway?" she asked. "Why am I stuck to it?"

"We've got a little lab here in the building," Brightly said. "And in it, we've developed a magnetic force strong enough to overpower the human body." He smirked. "If you think that's strong, you should feel it when I crank it up a few notches."

"No thanks," she said.

Brightly pushed up his glasses. "All right. Let's move on to our next round of tests. For these, we're gonna need you to be completely honest."

"I'm not doing any more of your stupid tests."

"Aww," Brightly said. "That's too bad! I was gonna free up your arms for this one. But if you refuse to cooperate"—he shrugged—"I can't do it."

"Fine!" It would be nice to have the use of her arms

again. "But first I need something to eat—and some water."

A pleased expression spread across Brightly's face. "Subject experiences hunger and thirst. Make a note of that, Jane."

Six

Jane used controls on her electronic tablet to free Eden's arms from the grip of the magnetic force and pull the chair to an upright position; then Dr. Patrick Evans rolled a rectangular table over.

Jane left the room, then came back with a bowl of spaghetti Bolognese and a glass of water. She, Brightly, and Dr. Evans pulled up chairs and watched Eden scarf it down. It was the worst spaghetti that Eden had ever tasted, but she needed the fuel to stay strong and sharp.

Also, she didn't know when she'd have a chance to eat again.

The way they watched her, you'd think they'd never seen someone eat before. Jane tapped on her tablet throughout. Sometimes she whispered to Brightly, and he nodded thoughtfully.

Eden eyed them suspiciously as she sucked down the

last few strands of spaghetti. The room was so silent, it was like eating dinner back in the lamp.

She patted her lips with a napkin. "What's for dessert?"

"Jane?" Brightly said.

Jane nodded, cleared the plates from Eden's table, rolled it away, and exited the room again.

"Seriously? I get dessert?"

But when Jane reentered thirty seconds later, she wasn't carrying anything sweet—just a black briefcase. She sat down, popped it open, and pulled out two more tablets, which she handed to Patrick and Brightly.

"What's that for?" Eden asked, but no one answered. Jane snapped the briefcase closed.

"All righty then," Brightly said. "Let's get this show on the road. What's your name?" He crossed his legs and peered at her.

"Eden."

"Are you a genie?"

"Yes."

Though Patrick was taking notes on his tablet, Jane seemed to be watching something on hers. Brightly looked over at it and nodded.

"What is she looking at?"

"Why don't you just answer these questions, Eden. How old are you?"

"Twelve and a half."

He cocked his head. "Do you have a birthday?"

"*Duh*. I'm alive, aren't I?" For being on the cutting edge of technology, these people sure were slow.

"When is it?"

"January twenty-fifth."

"And when did you become a genie?"

Eden sighed. "When I was born. Obviously."

Brightly cupped his chin in his hand. "Have you been granting wishes since you were born?"

"You've got to be joking."

"Answer the question," Jane cut in. It was the first time she'd spoken. It sounded like her accent was American, too.

"Of course I haven't! How could a baby go to Earth and grant wishes?"

There was a pause as they all took copious notes.

"I can't believe this," Eden muttered. "It's like genies for dummies."

Brightly uncrossed his legs and leaned forward, putting his elbows on his thighs. "Did you grant three wishes for a man named Reginald Clarke approximately two years ago?"

"*Who?*"

"Reginald Clarke," Brightly repeated in his slow Southern drawl.

"I have no idea who that is. Friend of yours?"

Brightly turned to Jane and nodded. She started tapping on her tablet.

"You know, it would be great if you could tell me what all this is for. Or, better yet, skip past it and make your wishes."

But Brightly just smiled. Eden banged the back of her head on the cushioned headrest in frustration.

"This is Reginald Clarke."

An image had been projected on the wall: a photograph of a grizzled old man with dark skin and patchy gray fuzz for hair.

Eden recoiled. Even with the ludicrous amount of money she'd granted him, he hadn't fixed his rotting teeth.

"How do you know *him*?" she asked.

"So you *do* remember Mr. Clarke." Brightly sounded pleased.

"How could I forget? The beach bum who spends his whole pathetic life hunting for treasure." He'd become her third wisher when he summoned her to Jamaica. The only good thing that had come of that granting was that she'd seen the ocean for the first time.

"Mr. Clarke runs the best resort in Jamaica," Brightly said.

"I know," Eden snarled. "How do you think he got it?"

"I went there last year for a vacation," Brightly went on. "Jane sent me. She thought I could use a little rest and relaxation. Very thoughtful." He shot Jane a simpering smile. "One night, I got into a conversation with Mr. Clarke at the bar. When I meet other professionals who dominate their fields, I try to learn their stories—and the secrets of their success, if they have them." His fingers drummed on his leg. "Well, Mr. Clarke sure did. That night he told me an incredible story.

"He said that one morning, about a year earlier, he'd been walking on the beach, searchin' for jewelry dropped in the sand. At the time, that was what he did most days. Having grown up poor on the island, he'd learned to make a livin' off the carelessness of wealthy tourists. He'd beg, search for lost valuables, pick a pocket or two on occasion."

"What a gentleman," Eden said sarcastically.

"I respected his drive." When Brightly leaned forward, she could see the coldness lying beneath his good-guy veneer. "Anyone who rises to the top knows you've got to look out for yourself. No one else will." Brightly leaned back. "On this particular mornin', Mr. Clarke wandered into an area he didn't normally cover. There he found a treasure unlike any he'd seen before: an antique oil lamp, made of gold. Right away, he knew it was special. It looked like a genie lamp, straight out of myths and legends. So he rubbed it, and a genie appeared." Brightly pointed at her. "That genie was you."

"And when he told you this, you believed him?" Most mortals doubted anything they couldn't prove. That was how the lamp remained a mysterious myth throughout the course of thousands of grantings.

"Darlin'," Brightly said, "I've built my career by dreamin' up things that don't exist, and makin' them real. For me, believin' in what you can't see is essential." He cracked his knuckles. "Mr. Clarke had told dozens of people about the lamp, but I was the first one to take him at his word. After that, I made it my mission to find you. And now I've done it. Here you are." He beamed that huge white smile. It was disgusting how pleased with himself he was.

Still, Eden had to wonder . . .

"How?"

She hated listening to him boast, but she also couldn't help her curiosity. She'd never heard of anyone setting out to find the lamp and then managing to do it.

"Have you ever used a cell phone?" Brightly asked.

"Yeah." As of two weeks ago, it was true.

"Do you happen to know who made that phone?"

Eden tried to visualize the phone she'd been carrying around in New York. Suddenly she realized why Brightly's name sounded familiar: it was printed in small letters on the back.

"You did," she said. "Or your company, at least."

"Correct," he said. "Brightly Tech has the honor of producin' ninety-three percent of the world's cellular phones, as well as ninety-five percent of electronic tablets, eighty-four percent of MP3 players, and eighty-seven percent of personal computers." He reared back as if someone else had just recited the statistics, and he couldn't believe they were true. "Is that right, Jane?"

"Eighty-five percent of MP3 players," she said dryly.

"Eighty-five percent!" He shook his head. "That number keeps creepin' up."

Eden rolled her eyes. "What does that have to do with the lamp?"

"Well, since I'm in charge of all the phones, I get to find out what everybody's talkin' about all the time!"

Eden blinked in disbelief. "You listen to people's conversations? Is that legal?"

"Heck no." Brightly pointed at her. "You gonna report me?" He laughed loudly.

She shook her head. "Okay. So you heard someone say something about the lamp?"

"Well, not exactly. I couldn't very well listen to every conversation all over the whole world and wait for someone to say 'genie lamp,' could I?" He chuckled. "Come on, now. This is Brightly Tech. We rigged up a little system to flag mentions of oil lamps, genie lamps, genies. Jane here was in charge of checkin' them out. Eventually she caught somebody tellin' their friend about this weird lil' antique lamp they'd found. Lucky for us, they didn't put the pieces together—just had it sittin' on a shelf in the house, didn't even try givin' it a rub!" He grinned. "So Jane got there, offered to pay them more money than they thought it was worth, and was back here faster than a hot knife slicin' through butter."

Eden was horrified. "That's *not* the way the lamp is supposed to be found."

"Hee-hee!" Brightly giggled. "What can I say? It's a dog-eat-dog world out there!"

Eden swallowed. She needed to wrap this up fast.

"If you've been waiting to find the lamp for so long, I'm sure you've come up with amazing wishes."

"Eden." Brightly tapped his fingertips together and leaned forward. "After what you've learned about me tonight, do you really think my mind works like other people's?"

Eden sighed. She'd never met a mortal with such a high opinion of himself.

"To be honest with you," Brightly said, "I'm more interested in learnin' how the lamp works. Last thing I wanna do is *waste* those wishes."

"All right," Eden said. "So I'll help you. Give you

a genie's expertise, so you can maximize the results. How's that?"

Brightly shook his head, thinking. "Not good enough."

Eden sighed. "Well then *what*?"

"I'm thinkin', if I've got such a powerful tool in my hands, why limit myself to three wishes?"

"I'll tell you why. Because that's the rule."

Brightly, Jane, and Dr. Evans all leaned forward.

"The rule?" Brightly asked.

"Yep. Rule number one. Every person has a lifetime limit of three wishes. And don't even think about trying to wish for more wishes. Trust me, you wouldn't be the first. It doesn't work."

Brightly pondered that as the others took notes. "But what if I were to—"

"Wish for that rule to change? Can't do that. The rules don't change for anyone."

Stupid mortal. He thought because he had a big company with fancy facilities, he could outsmart the lamp. *Think again,* she thought with satisfaction.

"Are there other rules?" Jane asked.

"Yeah. Rule number two: You can't change anything from the past. All wishes have to be for the present or the future. And rule number three: Wording counts. You only get what you ask for."

Brightly's eyes were on Jane's tablet.

"What are you looking at on there?" Eden asked.

But again, they ignored her question.

"Where do you live?" Brightly asked.

Eden paused. There was no way she was telling them about New York, or Pepper.

"Where do you live, Eden?"

"Venezuela."

As soon as she said it, Jane's expression went sour. She nudged Brightly, and he glanced at the screen of her tablet.

"You're lyin'," he snarled.

Abruptly, Eden understood. "Is this a lie-detector test?"

He stood up and pointed at her. "Don't you lie to me! I *hate* it when people lie to me!"

"David, calm down," said Jane.

"You know I hate it when people lie to me!" Brightly's face had gone red, and the volume of his voice was rising.

Eden screamed as her arms slammed down to the armrests again. The magnetic force had reactivated. He must have used his tablet to make it happen.

"David," Jane said. Her voice was even and controlled.

"This little genie is a *liar*!"

"Sit down." Jane waited until he did, then turned and stared into his eyes. "Are you ready to focus?"

Grudgingly, Brightly nodded.

Eden was mystified. Jane had spoken to him like a parent would speak to a child—and he'd listened!

Brightly took a deep breath. "Eden. The sooner you cooperate, the sooner we'll be done with this test. But in order to get through it, you've got to tell us the truth."

Jane nodded encouragingly.

But Eden was done with being treated like a science experiment. "If you want me to be truthful, you have to do the same!" she said. "Have you got me hooked up to some kind of . . . polygraph machine?"

Brightly paused. "Not exactly," he said in his slow, drawn-out drawl.

"Not *exactly*? What does that mean?"

"We're developin' a *new* sorta polygraph. This one's far more comprehensive than the ones from before. It measures your deceit by assessin' speech patterns and tonalities in the voice—so there's no need to gauge anything on the body." Now, behind the giant lenses of his glasses, his eyes danced with excitement. "We call it the Brightly Veritas."

Eden shook her head fiercely. "Forget it. I'm done."

"But—"

"Unless you bring me the lamp."

Brightly fell silent.

"Until you bring me the lamp, I won't talk."

Brightly turned to Jane, who shrugged. The Veritas must have shown that she wasn't bluffing.

"All right," Brightly said. He broke into a toothy grin. "Why not! Jane, Patrick, let's go."

"Go where?" Eden asked. "You said you'd bring it here."

"Oh! Well, we actually can't bring it here—not at the moment." Brightly grinned. "But we *can* bring you to it."

Seven

Brightly and Jane led Eden down a broad hallway with white walls and fluorescent lights until they reached a large door that Patrick pushed open. On the other side was a room completely unlike the one they'd been in.

It was wide, deep, and almost completely dark. Across it stretched two long lab tables with black tops. The only light was a purple glow emanating from a small source that seemed to hover above the farthest table. A man in a lab coat stood by it.

"This way," Brightly said. Eden followed him toward the purple light, with Jane and Dr. Evans trailing behind them. Along the way, she checked out the tables. They were covered with brand-new, expensive-looking equipment: Bunsen burners, glass beakers, graduated cylinders, and thermometers. She even spotted a few black rectangular devices that she was pretty sure were lasers, based on what she'd learned from Xavier.

It appeared that they'd brought her to a fully decked-out physics lab. But why would the lamp be here?

As Brightly and Eden approached the glowing purple thing, the man in the lab coat looked alarmed. She could see now that it was Jean Luc, the man who'd taken the lamp away.

"Don't worry," Brightly said. "Eden insists on seeing her mother ship, but we won't interrupt your work."

His work? Eden wondered as they reached the table. What kind of work was he doing?

Now that they were close, she could see that the glowing purple thing was inside a spherical cage. The cage was made of black metal bars that wrapped around the purple glow in a spiral pattern. It sat on a platform that rose about a foot above the lab table's surface.

When Eden peered more closely, she saw that inside the cage, within the midst of the purple glow, was the solid gold oil lamp she'd called home until two weeks ago.

"Eden," Brightly said. "Your lamp."

"What's that purple light around it?"

"Nothing to be concerned about," Brightly said. "Just an ionic plasma shield."

"A *what*?"

"A plasma shield," he said proudly. "The plasma forms a protective barrier around the lamp, clinging to it with the aid of a double electric field."

"Like a force field?" Eden asked incredulously.

"Essentially, yes."

"But I thought those were only in stories!"

"Strange, I used to think the same thing about genies," Brightly said. His lips curled into a smirk. "When you're on the cuttin' edge of technology research, lots of things exist that the rest of the world would still call make-believe."

Eden had learned about plasma and its properties in Xavier's physics lessons. It was one of the four forms of matter, along with solids, liquids, and gases. Of the four, it was the most abundant form in the universe; but on Earth, it generally existed only in labs.

"But *why*?" Eden demanded.

Brightly was gazing absorbedly at the plasma-encased lamp. "It's a little precaution we took. We don't want any external interference while we're investigatin'."

Eden's breath grew shallow. Would her request for reentry work with plasma blocking the spout? Xavier and Goldie might not be able to see or hear through the telescope.

Still, she had to try.

"Request for reentry!" she cried desperately. "I need to go back!"

She squeezed her eyes closed, willing it to work. She longed to be back in New York, right by Pepper's side.

But when she opened her eyes, nothing had changed.

She was still in the lab. The plasma shield still covered the lamp. Brightly was staring at her in delighted fascination, and Jane was tapping on her tablet like mad.

"What in the world was that?" Brightly hooted. "Some kinda special genie trick? Guess it didn't work this time!"

Eden gritted her teeth. On to the next option. She shot her hand toward the lamp, right between the cage's bars.

"I wouldn't—" Brightly said.

But it was too late. As she tried to grab the lamp, pain electrified her. It shot from her fingertips through her whole body, lighting her bones on fire. She howled in anguish.

Suddenly, something Xavier had once said popped into her mind: that the surface of the sun was a prime example of plasma. That meant this shield was the same temperature as the sun's surface.

Eden had no doubt that if she were mortal, it would have melted her hand off.

"Jane, make a note of that," Brightly said. He was interested in Eden's agony, but unconcerned by it. "Even when subject experiences pain of a very high degree, she suffers no damage to her body."

Tears rolled down Eden's cheeks. The excruciating pain was fading, but the sense of hopelessness replacing it was even worse.

Brightly rubbed his hands together. "Well, that was exciting! But now, please join me as we return to the examination."

He took Eden's elbow roughly and pulled her away from the lab table.

"Wait!" Eden racked her brain for a solution. She'd do absolutely anything to stay out of that chair.

"You want to try again?" Brightly asked. He crossed his arms and looked at her amusedly. "Be my guest."

"What are those?" she asked, pointing to four cylinders lined up against the wall behind Brightly and the others. They were approximately three feet tall, covered in silver, and topped with a stripe of green. On top of the green section were spouts.

Brightly sighed, but didn't turn around. "Eden, I know there are lots of interesting things in the lab, but let's not—"

"Just there, against the wall," she said. As they all turned to see what she was referring to, she took hold of an object she'd been eying on the table next to her.

"Those are oxygen tanks," Brightly said.

"Oh, good." As she said it, she swept up the black rectangle she'd wrapped her fingers around, aimed it toward the tanks, and squeezed. When she did, a purple laser shot out.

One of the tanks exploded with a loud crack and ignited. The flames danced outward and set the other tanks off too, causing three more earsplitting explosions in rapid succession, and a whole lot of fire in their wake.

Meanwhile, Brightly started to shriek—but not because of the fire. He was doubled over, gripping his leg a few inches above the knee. It seemed his thigh had been in the path of Eden's laser, and the beam had given it a nasty burn.

Patrick rushed to help Brightly, while Jane and the lab technicians scrambled to grab fire extinguishers. But Eden was already aiming the laser at the wall on the opposite side of the lab table. She swooped it in a wide circular motion. Running forward, she kicked the section of wall a few times inside the jagged circle she'd cut. It detached from the material around it and fell out into the space beyond.

Dropping the laser, she jumped through the hole.

The fall was much farther than she'd expected. As she flew through the night sky, her legs kicked under her in expectation of the ground that wouldn't come.

Finally, it did. She landed hard on her knees, feeling the crunch of her impact on the pavement. Fortunately, the power of her genie bracelet ensured that her limbs remained unharmed.

Brimming with adrenaline, she started to run. She didn't even look back to see if the lab had survived; all that mattered was that she had.

Eight

Pepper sat on her stool by the window and stared out at 44th Street. Lazy raindrops dripped down the glass pane, blurring the lit-up street outside. She hadn't moved for hours.

After Eden's disappearance, she'd made a quick exit from Tra La La Karaoke. She told her friends it was Eden's bedtime, and stole away before they noticed that the girl was already gone.

Rather than hailing a cab or taking the subway, she'd decided to walk. With every step, she'd anticipated Eden's return. Her little genie was sure to come back with a good story.

Once Eden was back, either Xavier or Goldie would arrive for the post-granting assessment. Pepper couldn't wait to see one of the masters in the flesh. Maybe, she thought, they could all duck into a diner together and have a late-night New

York dinner while they caught up on the past few centuries.

She'd walked the whole way home—from the East Village, through Gramercy Park, then up Broadway, crossing through Koreatown and gazing up fondly at the Empire State Building where she and Eden had first met. By the time she hit Times Square, with its giant blinking billboards, a misty rain was beginning to fall. When she finally reached her apartment building, her dress was soaked and her hair had frizzed up into a ball of wild, wet curls.

And Eden was still gone.

Another hour had passed since then, but Pepper was *still* alone. She sat in her darkened apartment, nails bitten to the quick, worry festering like acid in her stomach.

It had been too long.

During Pepper's genie career, only her granting with Shakespeare had taken more than an hour. (Two hours and thirteen minutes, to be exact.) Most grantings were over in ten minutes. It was astonishing how quickly mortals barreled through their wishes.

Once upon a time, Pepper had received a comprehensive education in the lamp, just like Eden and every other resident genie. Thinking back to Goldie's Lamp History lessons, Pepper remembered learning about the longest granting on record. In 1022 BC, a genie named Shadow had been summoned to a region that would now be called Uganda. Her wisher had promptly fainted with shock—not an unusual reaction for mortals. But while most wishers were revived quickly, this one hadn't come to for hours.

Of course, when he did wake up, he whizzed through his wishes without any further ado. Shadow was back in the lamp in a snap, with a total granting time of three hours and ten minutes.

Eden had been summoned at 8:15 P.M. According to the clock on Pepper's cell phone, it was now 11:07. Already, this granting had lasted for nearly as long as Shadow's.

Pepper wished she had a telescope like the one the masters used, so she could watch Eden's granting for herself. With a pang of anxiety, she hoped the wisher wasn't being rude or pushy. Though—knowing Eden—it was more likely that the genie was the one causing trouble.

She curled her toes around the rung at the bottom of her stool. If anything were amiss, she reasoned, the masters would send her a message to let her know what was going on. Still, that didn't ease her apprehension.

Looking after Eden was the only thing Xavier and Goldie had asked of her since she'd retired—and, thus, the most important task of her immortal life. For Pepper, to be chosen for this role was both a shock and a great honor. Unlike some of the alumni, she had never been a mother. But she imagined that parents must have to shoulder this vast sense of dread any time they didn't know where their children were.

She had no more fingernails left to bite, so Pepper chewed on a cuticle. Why on Earth wasn't Eden back?

She couldn't bear it one moment longer. She hopped off the stool, went to her bedside table, and tore a piece of parchment paper off the roll she kept in the drawer. She sat on the bed and held the paper in front of her face.

"Goldie, Xavier? It's me. I was thinking...Eden's been on this granting for an awfully long time. Could you fill me in on how it's going?" She forced herself to smile, pretending she was playing a role onstage. "I'm sure everything's fine. Just wanted to make sure. Anyway. Let me know." She rolled up the paper and gave it a squeeze.

But the paper didn't go anywhere.

She frowned and squeezed it again. Still nothing.

Pepper swallowed. Her pulse was starting to pound. Before Eden came to Earth, she rarely exchanged messages with the masters. But in the past two weeks, updates had flown back and forth between them as easily as mortals' e-mails. Every other time, Pepper had squeezed the parchment paper just like this. Every other time, it had worked.

She closed her eyes and hoped. She mustered all the positive energy she possibly could, believed with her whole heart that this time it would work, and gave the paper one more squeeze.

But it remained in her hand. By now it was crushed and crumpled, but it clearly wasn't going anywhere.

"Oh no," Pepper said out loud. "This is bad. This is very bad."

She crept back over to the stool. With a trembling hand, she set the parchment paper on the windowsill. The messaging system between the masters and alumni was one of the lamp's most basic magical powers. But that magic didn't seem to be working. *What was going on?*

She turned her eyes, filling fast with tears, to the brown leather backpack hanging from the coatrack. Inside it were Eden's passport and all her money. Eden's cell phone sat on the tiny kitchen counter, plugged into the charger. She was always forgetting to bring it with her, but it never mattered; Pepper was always by her side. Until now.

She wiped away a tear and took in a ragged breath. Then she picked up her own cell phone.

Somewhere among their instructions about looking after Eden, Xavier and Goldie had told her who to contact in case of an emergency they couldn't help with. At the time, Pepper couldn't imagine what sort of scenario that could possibly be.

She took a deep breath and opened her e-mails. She'd ignored several urgent calls to action that Bola had blasted out to all the Loyals (even less-active ones like herself) when Eden was in San Diego. Pepper had decided long ago to stay out of the struggle between the Loyals and the Electric as best she could, so it had been centuries since she'd communicated with their fierce (and, let's face it, frightening) leader. But it was Bola whom the masters had said to call in case of an emergency. Bola didn't know that Eden was on Earth, so Pepper would have to explain everything, they'd told her.

Pepper sighed. Desperate times call for desperate measures, she told herself. She pressed the phone number on Bola's e-mail.

"Yes?" The phone didn't even ring before Bola's sharp British accent hissed across the line. "Yes? Who is this?"

"It's Pepper." She cleared her throat. "Pepper, in New York."

"Yes, Pepper, I know where you are." Bola sounded annoyed. "Look, you're two weeks late. The genie's back in the lamp; the masters are safe. Case closed."

"I know that—"

"We could have used your help, you know. A show of support, if nothing else. But never mind that now."

"Well, actually—"

"Why are you calling me?" The coldness of Bola's tone made Pepper consider hanging up for a split second. But what then?

"I need your help."

"Mmm-hmm." Bola sounded distracted.

"Two weeks ago, the masters sent Eden to live on Earth, and they asked me to be her guardian. And everything was going really well, but then tonight she was summoned, and now it's been almost three hours, and that's too long for a granting. And I'm worried, I'm really worried."

"What? Pepper, you're not making sense. Start over, and speak articulately. The masters did *what*?"

Pepper took a deep breath. "Two weeks ago, after Eden returned to the lamp, Xavier and Goldie decided to let her live on Earth for the rest of her career. See, she's different from the rest of us. She wasn't happy there."

"They did *what*?"

"And they asked me to be her guardian."

"Her *guardian*?" Bola thundered. She barked a sound that Pepper assumed was meant to be some sort of laugh. "Pepper, this story is simply not plausible. Why would they allow her to live on Earth? And under *your* care?"

Pepper stiffened at the insult. "Why *not* my care?"

"I just don't understand why they would do that."

"Well, they did." Now Pepper was annoyed. "She's been here with me in New York for the past two weeks."

"I'm going to need to discuss this with them. I'll call you back."

"You can't!" Pepper said. "That's the other problem. My messages aren't sending. I think something's happened to the lamp."

The silence that followed felt like it was radioactively charged. Pepper could practically feel electrons ionizing.

"What. Do. You. Mean?" Bola shot the words across the line like bullets.

"I just tried sending a message to them, but it's useless. The magic isn't working." Pepper's voice broke on the last word.

Bola paused. "Let me call you back." And the line went dead.

Pepper's hand fell to her side. Her phone felt too heavy to hold.

Maybe, she thought, Bola would get through to them. Maybe there was something wrong with this piece of parchment. Maybe the trouble gathering around Pepper like a storm cloud would simply lift away. . . .

Her phone rang.

"You're right," Bola said. "It isn't working."

Pepper squeezed her eyes closed.

"I need to think," Bola said.

Pepper opened her eyes again. "Think about what?"

"I'll call you later."

"But—"

"Goodbye, Pepper." Suddenly, Bola was no longer on the line.

Pepper looked out at 44th Street. She pulled her knees up to her chest and watched as the rain started falling harder. For some reason, now that the problem was no longer hers alone, she was even more afraid.

If only she knew where Eden was! She'd go anywhere and do whatever it took to save her. But Eden might have been summoned to anywhere in the world, and at the moment, there was no way to know where.

There was nothing to do but wait, and keep hoping for her to turn up.

Nine

Eden raced down the street blindly, thinking of nothing except putting distance between her and that lab. She had no idea where in the world she was, let alone where she was going. All she knew was that she couldn't let them catch her.

Day hadn't yet broken, but it would soon; the sky was tinted with the reverse twilight between dark and dawn. Because of the early hour, almost no one was out—just a handful of sad souls asleep on the sidewalk. As Eden sprinted, she spotted a worn-out fedora lying on top of a pile of garbage. If anyone from Brightly Tech was looking, she'd be hard to miss when the streets were so empty. Still, it couldn't hurt to change *something* about her appearance. She scooped up the hat, then shoved it on her head and stuffed her long ponytail inside.

She tore through winding streets and alleys,

selecting them at random. It was lucky that whatever city she was in had lots of them. For it was a city— of that, she was certain. Wherever she was lacked Manhattan's up-all-night energy, but closed shops and cafés lined the streets.

She'd never had a reason to run this fast before, and it turned out it wasn't easy. Pain was shooting through her legs, and every breath was like a knife stabbing her chest. Even worse was the ache in her heart that came when she thought about Xavier and Goldie.

The plasma shield had blocked her masters' only portal to the world. That meant their view through the telescope was blacked out, and the messages that normally went in and out of the lamp wouldn't be able to get through. Brightly's technology had left Eden's masters not only helpless, but clueless.

But that wasn't the only problem. When Eden thought about what had just transpired, her mind went numb. She'd escaped from a wisher in the middle of a granting. She'd burned the wisher with a laser and set fire to his lab. And she'd left the lamp behind, at the mercy of that horrible mortal and his cohorts. That is, if they'd survived the fire.

At the thought of that, her skin went cold. Could the fire have *killed* one of those mortals? They were terrible people, but she didn't want to be responsible for their deaths!

Suddenly, it was all too much to bear. She had to stop running; her body couldn't take any more. She leaned against a building, put her hands on her knees, and took in giant gulps of air.

Looking down, she caught a glimpse of her gold cuff bracelet. It gave her a welcome wave of reassurance. As long as that bracelet was on her wrist, nothing could happen to her or her masters. It was a symbol of hope she could rely on, even when she didn't feel that hope.

By now, the sun had risen completely. People setting out for work or school were starting to populate the sidewalks. She'd look like a maniac if she started running again.

Get a grip, she told herself. *Think*. She took a deep breath and assessed her surroundings.

The streets were smaller than in New York, and they had a different feel. In Manhattan, it was as if every building strived to outdo all the others. But here, a quiet elegance graced the architecture. The buildings were shorter and stouter, older, and more pleasing to the eye. Things coordinated. Even the colors seemed to be painted from the same palette: taupe, tan, peach, yellow, a muted turquoise. The result was a coherent, unforced beauty, quite different from what she'd left behind.

Across the street was a blue street sign with white writing and a green border. Frowning, she read what it said: RUE GALANDE. And in the curved section on top: 5TH ARR.

Rue was the French word for "street." And *Arr.* stood for *arrondissement*, the term for a district in a French city.

Eden turned the corner and walked slowly up the street. Suspicion seeped through her mind like flavor from a tea bag.

As she reached the end of the street, church bells clanged to announce a new hour. When she saw what lay ahead, she gasped.

Across the street was a glistening river. It stretched to the left and the right as far as she could see, with bridges crossing it at periodic points. And on the other side of the river was the church that the bells were chiming from.

But it wasn't just any church. It was the Cathédrale Notre Dame.

Naturally, Eden had studied Notre Dame in the lamp. It was one of the world's most famous cathedrals, and a prominent example of French Gothic architecture. When she'd been trapped within the confines of the lamp's lesson room, she'd yearned to see it in person. But today, the sight had a different effect on her.

"You've got to be *kidding* me," she whispered.

The Cathédrale Notre Dame was in Paris. That meant *she* was in Paris.

And Paris was the location of Electra's headquarters.

Paris. As if it weren't bad enough to have a fuming, power-hungry tech genius on her trail, now she'd have to evade Sylvana and her pack of evil employees too. After the way she'd foiled them in San Diego, Eden could only imagine how thrilled they'd be to happen upon her roaming the streets of their city.

She rounded the corner and used the glass of a storefront as a mirror. She pulled the hat a little farther down on her head. Sure, it obscured her face a little—but if she were to cross paths with one of the Electric, there was a good chance they'd still recognize her.

The store in front of her was closed, but inside were shelves filled with thousands of books. She looked up and saw its name: Shakespeare and Company.

Eden's chest clenched tightly. Naturally, Shakespeare's name made her think of Pepper.

What would Pepper be doing right now, anyway? Did she think it was strange that the granting was lasting so long? Was she worried?

With a sensation like a rip through her heart, Eden remembered the tickets to *My Fair Lady*. They were supposed to go tonight.

Eden turned to face the river. She needed somewhere quiet and safe to think. Churches were supposed to be good for that, weren't they?

She crossed the closest bridge to reach the Île de la Cité, the small island that Notre Dame sat on. It was surrounded on all sides by the Seine, which curled through the center of Paris.

Even though the clock had just struck 8 A.M., mortals were already lined up waiting to enter. Instead of joining them, she walked around the side of the cathedral and saw patches of grass and manicured flower beds in the back. She found an empty bench, lay on her back across its seat, and closed her eyes.

She needed to get out of town—and fast. But she had no money, and she didn't have her passport—so even *with* money, she wouldn't be able to get back to the U.S. And since she hadn't brought her cell phone, she had no way to contact Pepper.

But anyway, she'd be crazy to get on the phone after learning how Brightly monitored phone calls. Assuming they'd survived the fire, Jane was probably already flagging phone conversations that included mentions of her name.

Despair flared in Eden's stomach. But just before it took hold of her, she caught herself.

The last time she was on Earth, the challenges she'd

faced had seemed insurmountable. And yet, she'd ended up right where she belonged. She didn't know how, but she'd get through this too. She'd simply have to. Because no one—mortal or immortal, no matter how rich or powerful—was going to steal her new life.

"Cool style," said someone in French.

Eden opened her eyes and saw a girl standing over her. Her thick dark hair was cut into a messy bob, with long bangs swept to one side. She was wearing suspenders over a men's oxford shirt with the sleeves roughly cut off. They were connected to tight, high-waisted jean shorts. Though she looked like she was around Eden's age, a slender silver ring pierced one of her nostrils. And on a strap around her neck was an expensive-looking camera.

"Merci," Eden replied—though she wasn't sure whether she considered it a compliment, coming from someone wearing such a strange outfit. She sat up to a cross-legged position.

"I mean, the dress—fine. But your hat," the girl continued in French. "I love it. Where's it from?"

"Uh..." Eden touched the fedora on her head. All morning she'd been inhaling a spicy, sort of rotten stench, and she was pretty sure the hat was its source—but she didn't dare take it off. "I found it on the street."

"Nice." The girl nodded, as if this were a perfectly normal way to acquire clothes. "You have school today?"

Eden supposed that, sprawled out on a bench wearing a hat that belonged in the trash, she must look more like a local than a tourist. Not quite the impression she'd had about Parisians.

"I'm skipping it," she answered. "You?"

"Nice." The girl maintained a calculated level of nonchalance, but Eden could tell she'd piqued her interest. "Maman and Papa homeschool me," she said. "But they're also professors at the Sorbonne, and they both have classes this morning. That means I get to do my work." She indicated the camera around her neck. "Can I take a photo of you in that hat for my blog?"

"No," Eden said hurriedly. "I should go."

"Oh, come on. You're skipping. You've got all day, right?" The girl sat next to Eden on the bench, pulled out her phone, and tapped the surface a few times. It, too, was a Brightly phone.

She held up the screen for Eden to see. "This is my blog. I take pictures of cool fashions I see around the city." She scrolled through photos of people wearing bizarre combinations of clothing.

Eden scrunched up her nose. The girl's idea of cool fashion was very different from her own.

However, seeing the blog gave her an idea.

"That's on the Internet, right?"

The girl gave her a strange look. "Yes, blogs are on the Internet."

That first night in New York, Pepper had used the Internet to find profile pages for Sasha and Tyler. Eden knew it wouldn't be wise to call Pepper, but maybe there was another way to contact her.

"What do you think?" the dark-haired girl asked. "Want to be on it?"

"No," Eden said. The girl's face fell. "It's a really nice blog," Eden assured her. "But today's not a good day for me to have my photo on the Internet. I need to fly under the radar."

The girl chewed on a fingernail. "Why? Because you're skipping school?"

Eden hoped the girl's curiosity would make her willing to help. "What's your name?" she asked.

"Melodie. And you?"

"Eden. Nice to meet you."

"Enchantée."

"Can I tell you a secret, Melodie?"

Melodie's eyes lit up. As she nodded, Eden could tell she was trying not to look overly eager.

"I ran away from home this morning."

Melodie gasped. "Ran away! Why?"

"It's hard to explain. Suffice to say, it was a bad situation."

Color was rushing to Melodie's cheeks. "That's so cool." She looked around to make sure no one was listening. "I've thought about running away," she confessed.

"Really?"

"*Oui.* My parents don't let me do *anything*. They ground me *all* the time. They're *awful*."

"I'm glad you understand," said Eden. It didn't really sound like a comparable situation—but the important thing was that she sympathized. "Actually, I wonder if you can help me. I need to get in touch with a friend."

"Don't you have a phone?"

"Not with me. I left in a rush. There was no time to take anything."

Melodie held out her phone. "*Pas de problème.* Use mine."

But as soon as it was in Eden's hand, she realized this was going to be tricky. Although she *had* a phone in New York, she almost never used it—and never to access the Internet. She tapped different symbols on the screen, but she didn't get anywhere. And all the while, she was acutely aware of Melodie watching her struggle.

"Actually, this might take a while." Eden thrust the phone back at her. "I don't want to use up your battery. Do you know where I might find a computer? One with the Internet on it."

Melodie touched the ring in her nose. Eden could see she was puzzled but intrigued. Melodie checked the chunky silver watch on her wrist.

"The Sorbonne Library is about to open. It's a few blocks away. You can use one there."

"Do I need money?"

"*Non*. You do need a membership, but I've got one. I can take you."

"Thanks," said Eden gratefully.

Ten

The library was one of several yellowy stone buildings that wore the name of the Sorbonne proudly engraved across them. It had the same classical elegance as many of the other buildings Eden had seen during her sprint across the city.

Melodie led her through the front gates, then across a wide courtyard. She showed her card to a series of security guards, then led Eden up some stairs into a stunning reading room.

Several long wooden tables crossed the room. They were lit by lamps with brass stands and green globes. The ceiling was covered with gorgeous paintings, and bookshelves lined the walls.

Actually, the room looked like it would fit quite well back in Eden's lamp—with the exception of the windows, of course. There were eight of them, spaced along the far wall with bookshelves between them. In front of each window was a computer.

They went to one, and Melodie used her information to log on.

"I'm going to look at art books," she said, and wandered off.

When she was gone, Eden sighed with relief. This would have been tough with Melodie watching over her shoulder. After all, it was her first time ever using a computer.

She squinted at the screen and cracked her knuckles. First, she needed to access the Internet.

She placed her hand on the mouse. From the line of icons at the bottom of the screen, a blue capital *W* looked like a good place to start.

She rolled the mouse to point the arrow on it and clicked. Nothing happened, so she clicked a few more times in rapid succession. This time a white rectangle spread across the screen.

Was this the Internet? Eden wasn't sure.

That night on the roof, Pepper had found Tyler's profile by typing his full name and the city where he lived. Somehow, she'd gotten the Internet to search for it. Eden scrutinized the computer's keyboard. Painstakingly, she sought out the letters to spell "Quincy Abbott New York City," pecking the keys one by one with her index fingers.

She stared at the screen. With the exception of the words she'd typed, it remained blank.

She saw a key on the keyboard with the word ENTER printed on it. She pressed it, but the only thing that changed was that the blinking vertical line moved down to the space below her words.

Maybe this wasn't the Internet.

Next to the *W* icon were a capital *O*, *P*, and *X*, but she skipped over them, opting to try a compass icon further down the line. She clicked it several times in succession, and now a new box took over the screen. An introductory page about the library occupied most of the space, but hovering above it was a long, narrow rectangular box.

She clicked inside the box and typed the words again. *Quincy Abbott New York City.* She pressed enter.

The first thing she saw was a photo of her guardian. Pepper's smile was so bright, it beamed out from the screen. Eden nearly cheered out loud!

When she clicked on the photo, she saw the Web site Pepper had shown her with profiles for different people. Slowly, with a good deal of trial and error, Eden created her own profile—with a fake name, of course. She might not be tech-savvy, but she wasn't stupid.

Once she'd set up her profile, she messaged Pepper.

Pepper, it's Eden, she typed. *I'm in Paris, and I'm in trouble. Can you come here? Bring my passport so we can go back to New York together once everything here has been fixed.*

She chewed her thumbnail for a moment. It was a lot to ask, she supposed—but she couldn't think of any other solution.

I'm sorry we missed My Fair Lady. *I'd do anything to be there.*

She waited for a minute, hoping a response would magically appear—but nothing happened. She checked the time on the computer screen: 9:27 A.M. She did a quick calculation in her mind. Paris's time zone was six hours ahead of New York's, so it was 3:27 A.M. there. Pepper was probably asleep.

There was only one other possibility. Since she was here, Eden thought, she might as well give it a shot.

Sasha Rockwell San Diego, she typed into the search bar. Sasha's profile popped up, with her photo of her in her volleyball uniform. Eden stretched her fingers, then started the message.

Sasha, it's Eden—not the name on the profile. Ignore that.

I wanted to say that I'm sorry for everything that happened. You might not ever want to talk to me again, but I thought I'd try.

Anyway, I'm back on Earth. I'm living here now, actually—in New York. It's a long story. But at the moment, I'm in Paris, and I'm in trouble. I have no money and no passport. I don't know what to do. I wish you and Tyler were here and

Eden stopped typing, and her shoulders slumped.

How could Tyler and Sasha possibly help her? They didn't have money to go gallivanting to Europe. They'd never even left the country. And anyway, why would they want to help a girl who'd nearly gotten their father killed?

She erased the start of the last sentence and rewrote it.

I hope you and Tyler and your dad are well. Maybe I'll see you again someday.

She pressed send before she could think about it too hard.

On Sasha's profile was a link with Tyler's name. Eden clicked on it. Seeing his photo sent a shot of adrenaline through her.

Should she send him a message too?

Just then, a little box started blinking in the bottom right corner of the screen. The box said *Quincy Abbott*.

Quick as she could, Eden clicked it.

EDEN!!!!! Are you okay? You're in Paris? What's happening??

Eden's heart swelled to twice its size.

Pepper! she typed. *Yes, I'm okay. But I need to get out of here ASAP. Granting gone wrong.*

Typing was starting to feel more natural. She was catching on to this computer stuff. She was grateful for the enchantment that created more space in genies' heads for new information.

Gone wrong? What do you mean?? Pepper sent. Then, *I'll be on the first flight to Paris.*

Too much to explain, Eden typed. *And I don't have much time. I'll tell you in person.*

Just checked flights. My flight will land at 8 P.M. your time. Can you hold out till then?

Eden bit her lip. She supposed she'd have to. And after all, only the handful of people who'd been in Brightly's lab would be looking for her. Paris was a big city. Surely she could evade them for the rest of the day.

Of course, she wrote.

I can't wait to see you, kid, Pepper wrote. *Where should I meet you?*

I'm at the Sorbonne Library now. Somewhere I can walk to from here that's easy to find.

How about the Louvre? You know how there's the pyramid at the entrance? At 9 P.M. Okay?

She did know. In Art History, Xavier had spent six weeks covering each section of Paris's world-famous behemoth of an art museum. The glass pyramid that stood in the courtyard of the Louvre Palace and served as its main entrance was its most distinctive feature.

Got it, Eden wrote.

"Who's that?" Melodie asked in French. She'd come up behind Eden's chair. She made a purring sound. "Tyler Rockwell. He's cute."

Eden quickly closed out of the window. She'd

forgotten that Tyler's profile was on her screen for any-one to see.

"Is he going to come rescue you?" Melodie asked teasingly.

"No." Realizing how emphatically she'd said it, Eden forced herself to laugh. "He lives in California."

"You have friends in California?"

"Yeah."

"Cool." Melodie pushed her bangs behind her ear. "Did you talk to whoever *is* going to help you?"

"Oui."

"What's the plan?"

"We're meeting tonight." She'd just need to figure out how to get to the Louvre. But seeing as it was one of Paris's main attractions, it shouldn't be hard to get directions.

Melodie wiggled her eyebrows up and down. *"Quel mystère."* She looked at the computer. "Hey, since we're here, I need to print something. Can you wait for a second?"

Eden got up, and Melodie took her chair. More uni-versity students were sitting at the long tables. Eden stood by Melodie and watched them. Could she be one of them someday? Maybe she could even attend NYU or Columbia, and stay in New York with Pepper.

"Eden," Melodie hissed. She swiveled in her chair.

"What?"

Eden followed Melodie's eyes to the computer screen. On it was a news article with an unmissable headline.

BREAKING: DAVID BRIGHTLY SEARCHING FOR ADOPTED DAUGHTER, SUSPECTS KIDNAPPING

Accompanying it was a photo of Eden in her pink-and-white-striped dress. Somehow, they'd caught her at a moment when she didn't look petrified.

The text read:

Tech mastermind David Brightly has announced the disappearance of his adopted daughter, a 12-year-old named Eden.

"She's the most precious thing in my life," Brightly stated in a press release issued this morning.

Although based in the Silicon Valley, Brightly has spent the past few weeks in Paris conducting research for a highly confidential project.

The news came as a particular shock because Brightly has not disclosed his daughter's existence to the public until now.

Brightly explained that Eden was originally his niece, but he adopted her when his sister passed away several years ago.

"I wanted to protect her privacy," he said. "She's been through enough already."

Brightly asserted that he suspects the disappearance is the work of a kidnapper. He has promised a reward to anyone who can offer information as to her whereabouts.

As she read the words, Eden felt like she'd fallen through the floor into a bottomless hole. She kept sinking, and sinking, and sinking.

Melodie was gazing at her in awe.

"That's you," she whispered.

Eleven

Eden couldn't speak. Her vision went blurry as she looked around the library. Suddenly, every person was a threat.

Melodie logged out of the computer, then stood up abruptly.

"Come with me," she said.

But Eden knew better. She'd granted enough wishes to know how mortals behaved under the influence of money's bright, shiny lure.

"No," she said.

Melodie's eyes bulged. "Are you crazy? Do you *want* to get caught?"

Eden looked around anxiously. It probably *was* a good idea to go somewhere else. It was only a matter of time until someone here saw the news and recognized her.

"Okay," she relented. "Where?"

"Out of here, to begin with!"

Eden took a deep breath and nodded. Ducking her head, she followed Melodie downstairs, past the security guards, into the courtyard outside. Every glance that came her way singed like a hot match against her skin.

They reached an empty space at the edge of the courtyard and faced one another.

"You're *David Brightly's* daughter?"

"Do you know who he is?" Eden asked. Even though Brightly's name was on every phone she'd seen on Earth and his announcement had made headlines, it seemed impossible that his reputation could measure up to his ego.

"Are you kidding? *Everyone* knows who he is!" Melodie crossed her arms. "That was an important thing to leave out of the story you told me."

"Well, now you see why I wanted to stay under the radar," Eden said. She shrugged. "I told you, I ran away from home. It was a bad situation."

"But Eden!" Melodie hissed. "This is big-time! You're on the run!"

"Shhh!" Eden looked around wildly—but the student who'd just walked by them continued on obliviously.

"Look," Melodie whispered, "I can help you—if you want. My apartment is across the street. You can hide there for a while."

"Yeah, right," Eden said. "You'll turn me in!"

Bright pink spots appeared on Melodie's cheeks. "Do you think I'm some kind of jerk? I told you, I understand. I've thought about running away too!"

Eden took in Melodie's suspenders, her high-waisted shorts, the ring in her nose. What kind of twelve-year-old wore a nose ring?

In San Diego, just about everyone she'd encountered—mortal or immortal—had turned out to be different from how they'd first appeared. Gigi, also known as Genevieve, was a Loyal genie alum who'd posed as a seventh-grade bully. And although Sylvana had made herself out to be Eden's kindred spirit, that bubble had burst when her evil plan to seize the lamp's power came to light.

But on the other hand, Eden had been wary of Tyler and Sasha when she'd first met them, and they'd turned out to be good, true friends. They'd risked everything to help her.

Melodie was offering to be a friend to her, too. Could she be trusted?

"Brightly's offering a reward for information on me," Eden said. "Why would I believe you don't want that money?"

"Eden." Melodie put her hands on her hips. "I'm homeschooled. My parents are strict. My life is *boring*! I get in trouble every single day. And you know why?"

"Why?"

Melodie lifted her chin. "Because I am *une rebelle*! Always have been, always will be. What do I want money for if I can have adventure? Helping a girl on the run is like a dream come true for me. *Especially* the daughter of David Brightly."

Eden was torn. On the one hand, she could see that Melodie meant what she said. And the truth was, she could relate. Hadn't she escaped the lamp in search of adventure?

And yet . . . what if she took a risk trusting this girl, and wound up back in Brightly's clutches?

"You know what?" Melodie said. "Never mind. I wanted to help, but I can't make you trust me." She looked at Eden like she felt sorry for her. "I just hope you realize how hard this is going to be on your own. No offense, but you seem pretty clueless."

She turned and strode away.

As Eden watched her disappear through the gate, her stomach sank. How *would* she do this on her own?

There was no question that trusting Melodie would be a risk. But she was going to have to take a chance on *something*.

Eden ran through the courtyard's entrance to the sidewalk. "Melodie!"

Melodie had just reached the other side of the street. On the opposite sidewalk, she turned to face Eden.

"You're right," Eden said. "I need help. I'm coming with you."

At a stone building a few doors down, Melodie punched a code into a number pad and pushed the big wooden door open. Inside was a tight winding spiral staircase. However, instead of taking the stairs, Melodie opened a door to the tiniest elevator Eden had ever seen. It was a tight fit with both of them inside.

She pressed the button for the fourth floor, the elevator door slid closed, and with a jerk, they started to rise.

The elevator lurched to a stop, and the door slid open. Right in front of them was an old lady with a scarf wrapped around her head.

"Bonjour, Melodie," the old lady said. *"Comment vas-tu?"*

"Madame Babineaux!" Melodie said. *"Très bien, et vous?"*

The woman stared at Eden through tiny glasses. "Who is your friend?" she asked in French.

"I'll see you later!" Melodie said, squeezing past her.

"Melodie!" the lady called. "No trouble today, I hope!"

Melodie groaned as she stalked down the hall and let them into one of the apartments. "What did I tell you?" she said. "The walls here are thin, so when Maman and Papa yell at me, the whole building hears it."

The door opened to a small, tidy living room. Eden did a quick sweep of the space, but no one else seemed to be there. A blue armchair sat perpendicular to a brown sofa that was brightened by yellow and blue throw pillows. In front of it was a kidney-shaped coffee table, and on the opposite wall was a record player on a vintage cabinet.

The front room flowed into a kitchen. There was a cutout window with two pewter bar stools sitting in front of it. Through the window, Eden could see an old-fashioned powder-blue refrigerator.

The living room's walls were covered with framed French magazine covers and newspaper clippings. On one wall, a window opened to the courtyard. Eden went to it, leaned out, and inhaled a fresh breath of Parisian air.

She savored it as it filled her lungs.

"Want a cup of tea?" Melodie asked from the kitchen.

"Sure." Eden turned from the window.

"Actually, how about breakfast? Have you eaten?"

"No, not yet."

In truth, what she needed was sleep. She'd been awake since the night before Tra La La Karaoke. She'd been running (literally) off adrenaline. If she didn't get some rest soon, she was going to crash—and if it wasn't somewhere hidden, that would make her an easy target for anyone who wanted Brightly's reward. Which, she had to assume, was every person in Paris.

Eden walked along the wall, inspecting the magazine covers and newspaper clippings. She saw *Le Monde*,

Le Figaro, *L'Express*, and many others. Their dates ranged through the past few decades.

"Milk in your tea?" Melodie was watching Eden through the cutout window.

"Yes, please. What's with all these magazines?"

"My parents are journalists."

"I thought they were professors," said Eden.

"Well, that, too. They teach journalism at the Sorbonne."

Great. Her face was plastered all over the news, and she'd made her way into the home of two reporters.

Melodie slid two cups of steaming tea through the cutout window, followed by a plate of croissants. *"Voilà."*

Eden joined her and selected a *pain au chocolat* from the plate.

Melodie pulled the fedora off Eden's head, and her ponytail fell free. "There's the blond hair in that photo." She put the hat on her own head and ripped a piece off a croissant.

Eden pulled the elastic out of her ponytail to let her hair loose, and massaged her head with her fingers.

"I'm sorry about your mother," Melodie said.

"Thank you," Eden answered carefully, remembering what the news story had said. Allegedly, she was the daughter of Brightly's sister, who'd passed away a few years ago.

Melodie leaned forward on the counter and cupped

her chin in her hands. "Where did you live when she was alive?"

Eden swallowed a sip of tea. "New York City."

"New York City!" Melodie's expression grew wistful. "I've always wanted to go there!"

Eden told her about baseball games at Yankee Stadium, shopping in SoHo, and eating hot dogs in Central Park. She stretched her two weeks in New York into an imaginary first ten years of her life, inventing an alternate universe where Pepper was her now-deceased mother.

"She had a beautiful singing voice," she said. "Once a week, she'd bring me to a karaoke bar. She always sang a song just for me." Remembering Pepper performing their special song lifted Eden's spirits. She really couldn't wait to see her again.

"Your life sounds so exciting." Melodie's eyes shone with longing. Eden wondered what she'd think if she knew the *whole* truth. "So when she died, you moved to Silicon Valley with your uncle?"

"*Oui.*"

"I guess that's why you have friends in California." Melodie sized her up. "By the way, you speak French really well for an American."

"Oh really? Thanks," Eden said cautiously.

Melodie adjusted her suspenders. "How long have you been in Paris?"

"A few weeks."

"What school have you been going to?"

"I lied about that." Eden shrugged apologetically. "I have a private tutor. Like you, I guess."

Melodie tapped her fingers on the countertop. "Why do you think your uncle kept you a secret all this time?"

"Who knows?" Eden tried her hardest to seem natural.

The fedora cast a shadow over Melodie's face, making it hard to read her expression.

"Who did you message when we were at the library?"

"A friend. Like I told you."

"Is his name Tyler Rockwell?"

"No!" Eden said in dismay.

Melodie cackled. "You're blushing!"

"No I'm not!" But even as she said it, she felt heat in her cheeks.

"I'm not judging you. I'd run away with a boy too, if I could. Especially one who looks like *that*." Melodie winked. Eden was blushing so hard, she thought she might pass out.

"I swear, it's not Tyler who's coming. It's a friend of mine named Quincy. She's coming from New York."

"Okay. And you're meeting her—"

"Tonight."

Melodie put her hands on her hips. "Stop dancing around things. When and where?"

Eden swallowed. "The Louvre Pyramid. Nine P.M."

"Now we're getting somewhere." Melodie nodded. "My parents will be home at two P.M. You can stay here until then. But after that, you're going to need a disguise. All of Paris will be looking for you." She eyed Eden critically. "In the photo they released, you look exactly like you do now. You're just asking to get caught. You need to change out of that dress. And the long blond hair is a dead giveaway."

Eden touched it self-consciously.

"It was clever of you to pick up this hat." Melodie pulled it off and tossed it on the floor. "But it's not good enough. Plus, it smells like a toilet." She made a gagging face.

"What are you thinking?"

"I'm thinking you're lucky you met me." Melodie smirked. "Clothes are my specialty—and you're going to be my new project."

Twelve

In the lamp, Eden had grown up with an enormous closet filled with elegant dresses, luxurious furs, and finely crafted shoes. None of it had meant much to her; her favorite part was the back wall, where she'd tallied her granted wishes with an old tube of lipstick. She was far more concerned with her countdown to freedom than anything within the lamp's gold walls.

Now that she lived on Earth, she understood how rare it was to own such a large collection of clothing. In Mission Beach, Sasha's shorts, jeans, and tank tops had all fit into a dresser in her half of the room she shared with Tyler. And Pepper's clothes hung in a tiny closet in her studio apartment.

However, Melodie's wardrobe rivaled Eden's former closet—in size, at least. The content might have come from a different planet.

The closet itself didn't contain even half her clothes. They'd spilled out and overtaken her room. Wardrobe racks spanned the lengths of three of her walls, with her bed against the fourth. On the racks were clothes of every imaginable color, material, and style, including sequins, ruffles, leather, and animal print.

Thumbtacked to the wall space above the wardrobe racks were design sketches and pages ripped from fashion magazines. There were also dozens of hats hanging on pegs.

"Wow," Eden said. "You *do* love clothes."

"I told you." Melodie started to sift through the racks. "Now, what we've got to do is find something that looks like the opposite of anything you'd ever wear."

"Isn't the point for me to go unnoticed?" In Eden's line of sight were an orange jumpsuit that looked like a prison uniform, a shiny green skirt like a mermaid's tail, and a feathered Native American headdress. "I don't think I'd blend in wearing most of this stuff."

"We'll put you in something subtle."

Taking it all in, Eden wondered where exactly Melodie planned to find that.

Though Melodie's wardrobe seemed chaotically disorganized from an outsider's perspective, *she* seemed to know precisely where everything was. After careful consideration, she pulled out a white collared shirt, a navy blazer, a pleated green-and-navy skirt, shiny black shoes, and a navy beret to top it all off. Eden put all of it on as instructed.

"See?" Melodie said delightedly. "You're just a regular student in Paris!"

Eden examined herself in the full-length mirror on the closet door. She had to admit, she did look pretty normal. There was just one problem. "But you can still see my hair."

Melodie frowned. "Hmm..." She snapped her fingers. "I've got it! I know just what you need. But I have to go to a store to buy it. Can you wait here?"

Eden didn't say anything. What if Melodie was planning to go somewhere and turn her in?

"After all this, you still don't trust me?" Melodie shook her head. "I'll leave my phone here so you know I'm not making any sneaky calls. Okay?"

"Okay."

"I'll be back soon!" she called on her way out the door.

Eden cleared a polka-dot dress off Melodie's bed to make space, then lay back on the pillows. She seriously hoped Melodie was right that this disguise would keep her safe until Pepper arrived.

But what then? As much as Eden would love to turn around and go back to New York, they couldn't do that.

Xavier and Goldie were in serious danger. They had to get the lamp back from Brightly.

The problem was, she had no idea how. It would be insane for her to go anywhere near Brightly Tech when he was scouring the city for her.

Eden frowned at the ceiling. There had to be a chink in Brightly's armor, but it was hard to imagine what it could be. He had unlimited resources, and access to the world's most advanced technology. He was highly intelligent and extremely confident. Until Eden had escaped, he'd been completely in control. The only exception was when he'd caught her in a lie. He would have thrown a full-blown tantrum if Jane Johnston hadn't convinced him to simmer down.

It seemed that Jane's influence on Brightly was considerable. That might be important, Eden thought. Maybe it could help her somehow. But in order to find out how, she needed to know more about Jane and her relationship with Brightly.

She sat up and looked around the room. Melodie had left her phone on the nightstand next to her bed. Under it was a laptop computer.

"I'm back!" Melodie called as the front door slammed. She came into the bedroom holding a plastic bag. Reaching in, she pulled out what looked like a small animal.

"Ew," Eden said. "What's that?"

"Your secret weapon. Can you put your hair in a low bun?"

Eden used the elastic around her wrist to secure her hair in a twisted knot at the nape of her neck. Melodie stood up and affixed the hairy brown thing to her head. Eden winced as she adjusted its stretchy, scratchy edges.

Next, Melodie fitted the navy beret on top. She took a step back to evaluate.

"Voilà!" She clapped her hands. "You're no longer Eden Brightly!"

Eden turned to the mirror. For the first time in her life, she was a brunette. The wig now on her head was exactly like Melodie's hair: a dark-brown bob, with long, side-swept bangs.

The hair made her whole face look different. She looked slightly older, and more serious and sophisticated. Her skin seemed paler, and her eyes were bluer and more piercing.

"It suits you," Melodie said. She pulled another wig out of the bag. This one was neon orange and shoulder-length. "This one's for me," she said slyly as she put it on. She whistled when she saw herself in the mirror. "Hot like fire."

"How long before your parents are home?" Eden asked.

Melodie checked her watch again. "About an hour."

"Before I go, can I use your computer?" Eden was thinking she could use the Internet to search for information on Jane. She might as well check her messages, too. She didn't really expect a response from Sasha, but it couldn't hurt to check.

Melodie handed the laptop to Eden. "All yours."

"Thanks." Eden opened it and was happy to see the same symbol that had taken her to the Internet in the library. As she clicked it, she decided it was safe to tell Melodie a little more of the truth. "My uncle can monitor calls on Brightly phones, so I don't want to call my friend," she explained. "I'm scared he'd be able to track me down."

"Wow," Melodie breathed. *"C'est grave."*

"That's why I'm sticking to messages on the Internet."

"Um...Eden? Did you leave your common sense at home too?"

Eden paused and looked up from the computer. "What do you mean?"

Melodie sat next to her on the bed. "Your uncle basically *controls* the Internet. If he can monitor phone calls, he can definitely monitor things online."

Apprehension rippled through Eden. "You think so?"
"Yes!"

Her skin started tingling with fear. Why hadn't she thought of that?

Melodie shook her head in confusion. "I don't

understand how you're so clueless about technology when you live with David Brightly."

"I guess I wasn't thinking." Eden breathed deeply, trying not to panic.

Melodie tucked her hair behind her ear. "Let's stay calm. In the message you wrote at the library, did you say when and where you were meeting your friend?"

"Yes. But I sent it from a fake profile."

"Okay, that's good. Your real name wasn't anywhere in the messages?"

Eden thought back and winced. "It was."

If Brightly or Jane saw those messages, they'd see that she was planning to meet Pepper at 9 P.M. at the Louvre Pyramid. They'd also see that she'd been at the Sorbonne Library this morning. What if they went looking for her there? It was just across the street.

Eden jumped up. "I need to get out of here."

"I think you're right," Melodie said. "My parents will be home before long anyway. And even if you weren't on the run, I'd be in big trouble for having you here."

"Why?"

"Technically, I'm grounded this week. I'm not supposed to have friends over. Oh! I almost forgot." She reached into the plastic bag again. This time, she pulled out a pair of mirrored sunglasses with round lenses. "One final touch."

When Eden put them on, her mirror image became almost unrecognizable.

"Perfect, right?"

"Not bad," Eden admitted.

"Now come on, let's go."

"You're coming too?"

"Mais oui," said Melodie. "You obviously need my help." She picked up her camera from the bed. "Anyway, I still need photos for my blog."

"But you're grounded. Doesn't that mean you're not supposed to leave home?"

"They can't do anything about it if they don't know where I am." Melodie's eyes sparkled with mischief. "Now come on. Let's go!"

As they left the apartment, purpose propelled Eden's steps. When they reached the tiny elevator, she ran right past it. With one smooth movement, she hopped on the banister and slid right down it, spiraling all the way to the bottom.

She'd known the skills she'd perfected in the lamp would come in handy someday.

Thirteen

Eden stayed in the lobby while Melodie went out to investigate. After a minute, she opened the big wooden door and slipped back in.

"There's a man standing outside the library with his arms crossed. Looks like he could be some kind of guard on watch."

"What does he look like?" Eden asked.

"Tall, blond. Kind of stiff-looking. About my parents' age, I guess."

Eden nodded. "I think I know him. He's one of Brightly's people."

"You call him Brightly?" Melodie frowned as she adjusted her orange wig.

Whoops, Eden thought. She shrugged. "He's not my *real* dad, you know."

Melodie lifted an eyebrow. "We'll go in the opposite

direction. Act casual." She opened the door and gestured for Eden to follow.

Once they were a safe distance away, Eden looked over her shoulder. Just as she'd suspected, the man keeping watch outside the library was Dr. Patrick Evans.

An unpleasant chill ran through her body. Could one of the others be inside? Jane Johnston? Even Brightly himself?

She jogged to catch up with Melodie.

"Did you get a look at him?" Melodie asked.

"*Oui*. It's who I thought it might be." Eden shook her head. "Good thing you stopped me before I started sending messages from your computer. They might have shown up at your apartment."

"Aren't you glad you believed me for once?" Melodie smirked. "By the way, where are we going?"

Eden adjusted her sunglasses. "I still need to search for that information." She was itching to learn more about Jane Johnston's relationship with Brightly. "Could we go to a different library? I'll be careful not to do anything that would trip Brightly's sensors."

Melodie seemed doubtful. "You think it's worth the risk? It would be safer to find somewhere for you to hide all day."

"I know," Eden said, "but I need to." She couldn't

explain to Melodie that she had to find a way to save the lamp and her masters. "I also have to change the location for tonight," she pointed out. "The fact that Brightly sent people to the Sorbonne Library means they definitely read my messages, and they would have seen the plans we set. They'll probably be waiting for me at the Louvre at nine."

"And even if you don't show, they'll be there waiting for your friend Quincy."

Eden shuddered at the thought. "Exactly."

"You can't send another message from that account, though," said Melodie. "They'll be waiting for you to log in again—and when you do, I bet they'll show up wherever you are."

"I know." Eden scratched her scalp. The wig was itchy, but at least it seemed to be working. So far, no one had given her a second glance.

Melodie snapped her fingers. "I know: we can message your friend from my account. We'll put it in code, so your uncle's people won't pick up on it."

"That's a good idea," Eden agreed. "But where can we do that? I don't think we should use your phone."

"True," Melodie agreed. "Anyway, I turned it off so my parents can't call me. Now I've got to stay under the radar too."

They turned into a narrow alley lined with small

storefronts. There were crêperies, gelato shops, gyro shops, and even a jazz club.

"Are you sure you want to do that?" Eden asked. "If your parents get home and see you're not there and then they can't reach you, won't they be really worried?"

Melodie laughed. "More like really mad! They know me well enough to expect I'll be out causing trouble somewhere. They'll be furious." She threw her shoulders back. "But I don't care. I'm not going to leave you now. Remember what I told you?"

Eden smiled. Melodie really was *une rebelle*—but it seemed she was also a loyal friend. Eden was glad she'd decided to trust her.

"Want to grab lunch?" Melodie asked. "These gyros are *magnifique*." She kissed her fingers dramatically.

Eden looked back over her shoulder. Dr. Evans hadn't seen her, but knowing he was so near made her anxious. "Do you think it's safe?"

"We'll buy them and keep moving," Melodie said. "We've got to eat, right?"

She bought one gyro for herself, and one for Eden. Eden watched in fascination as a man behind the counter took shavings off a massive cone of meat, striped with fat and rotating on a long stick. He wrapped the meat in pitas, along with lettuce, tomatoes, and tzatziki.

Eden took her first bite as they emerged from the alley. *"Yum,"* she said.

"What did I tell you?" said Melodie triumphantly. As they ate, she led them toward the river.

"So where can we use a computer?" Eden asked. "Another library?"

"Hmmm." Melodie touched her nose ring as she thought. "You know the Kiwi store on the Champs-Élysées?"

"Kiwi? As in the bird, or the fuzzy-skinned fruit?"

Melodie came to a sudden stop. The way her forehead crinkled in confusion let Eden know she'd said something wrong. "Kiwi, the brand. Don't you know it?"

"Um . . ."

"How could you not know the name of the only tech company in the world that's big enough to compete with your uncle's company?"

Eden's face went hot. "Oh, *that* Kiwi. Of course."

Melodie gazed at her intently, like she was searching for something. "You know, if I hadn't seen that photo, I wouldn't believe you're David Brightly's daughter."

Eden swallowed. "Adopted daughter."

"Whatever." Melodie shook her head quickly, as if to get rid of the thought, and started walking again. "Kiwi has a store on the Champs-Élysées. They always have computers on display. We can use one there."

"And Brightly won't be able to track it, because it won't be a Brightly computer!" Eden said excitedly.

"I wouldn't count on that," Melodie said. "But it's free to use them, and there's tons of turnover throughout the day. And it's better than walking into a Brightly store, don't you think?"

There was no arguing with that.

As Eden and Melodie walked along the Seine's south bank, boats loaded with smiling passengers cruised by. Parisian landmarks lined the river's banks like dignified members of a royal court, and between the bridges, the water glittered as if there were tiny lights beneath the surface. No two bridges were alike. They were made of steel, iron, stone, and wood. Some were for foot traffic only, while cars drove on others. On some of them, street performers played instruments.

There was so much to see that Eden kept getting distracted and falling behind, meaning Melodie kept having to wait for her to catch up. After this happened a few times, Melodie said, "You've seen all this, right? You've been in Paris for weeks."

"Even if I'd been here for years, I don't think I'd ever get used to this," Eden said.

"Trust me, you would." Melodie nodded toward the next bridge. "Let's cross here."

It was one of the bridges for pedestrians only. The plywood that covered the sides was painted with colorful designs.

"This is the bridge that used to have all the locks," Melodie said as they turned onto it.

"Locks?"

"You know. The sides were made of wire mesh, and people would come here and hook locks through them. They'd write their names or initials on them with the date. Couples that think they're going to stay together forever, you know?" Melodie snickered. "Good luck."

Eden tried to imagine what it had looked like. "Why don't they do it anymore?"

"The locks were too heavy. The bridge was going to collapse! They had to take them off and cover the sides with wood. You didn't know about this?"

Not long ago, Eden would have dismissed this as a typical move by dumb mortals. But at the moment, the idea of all those memories being torn down hit her differently. "That's kind of sad," she murmured.

"Sad? *Non*," said Melodie. "The whole thing was pretty stupid."

Up ahead, a majestic-looking tan building stretched along the river's opposite bank. As they approached it, Eden realized that she recognized it. They were walking toward the Louvre Palace.

They passed under an arch and into one of its

courtyards. Once inside, she turned in a circle, gazing in wonder at each side of the palace. It was even larger and grander than the mental image she'd formed during Xavier's lessons.

Melodie was clearly unimpressed. She must have seen it countless times to be so immune to its splendor.

"Come on." She beckoned Eden to another arch on the left side of the courtyard. "Through here."

Eden could have stayed staring for hours, but she also didn't mind moving ahead. After all, the adjacent courtyard was where the Louvre pyramid was located. Since she was no longer going to come here tonight, she was glad to have the chance to see it now.

The pyramid looked like a spaceship that had made an emergency landing. It was unique, but not exactly pleasing to the eye. Its sharp lines and glass panes made it look jarringly modern next to the palace.

It was also surrounded by throngs of tourists. Many of them queued up to get inside, while nearly as many others were using the one-of-a-kind backdrop as a photo op, standing on concrete blocks that stuck out of the ground with their arms held out. To their photographers, they would appear to be propped against the pyramid; but to anyone else, they looked ridiculous. Watching them, Eden had to laugh.

Melodie giggled too. "Silly, right?" She held up her camera and snapped a photo.

Just like in Times Square and the Empire State Building, people were speaking in dozens of languages. As they crossed the courtyard, Eden listened in on their conversations.

"Are we going to see the *Mona Lisa*?" a little girl asked her mother in Japanese.

"I'd like to have fish for dinner," said an elderly man in Spanish.

"They won't be here until nine P.M.?" a deep voice asked in French.

"That's when they planned to meet," a woman answered. "But we need eyes on the area all day in case she turns up earlier."

Abruptly, Eden turned toward the voices. Six men in suits were facing a petite woman whose brown hair was pulled into a low ponytail.

Eden recognized her immediately. It took every ounce of her self-control not to scream.

"Shouldn't some of us wait at the airport in case the girl tries to skip town?" asked one man.

"Didn't you listen to what I said?" Jane snapped. "She doesn't have money or a passport. Plus, we know for a fact that they're meeting here. And anyway, if she did go there, airport security would stop her."

Thankfully, Jane was facing away from Eden, and the men seemed oblivious that their target was strolling by right in front of them.

"Pick up the pace," Eden hissed to Melodie. "Brightly's people are here."

Melodie gawked. "You're serious?"

"Yes. Don't look. We've got to move."

Melodie took Eden's arm and steered them through purposefully. "Did they see you?"

"I don't think so." Eden didn't dare look in their direction again, for fear of attracting their attention.

"Don't worry," Melodie said. Eden tried not to hyperventilate as they beelined across. They exited the courtyard and crossed into the Tuileries, a wonderland of foliage, flowers, and fountains.

"Let's keep up the pace for a little bit longer," Eden murmured. "Just in case."

She'd learned about the history of the Tuileries in Xavier's lessons. It was created by Queen Catherine de Medici in 1564, and opened to the public in 1667. But Xavier hadn't told her about its amusement park rides. Up ahead was a Ferris wheel—and behind it, a ride with a long metal arm holding a carriage of mortals on each end. The mortals screamed as it rotated, spinning them up to the sky, then down to the ground.

The sight and the sounds opened a floodgate of disturbing memories. The last time Eden had seen Tyler and Sasha was in an amusement park in San Diego. She shivered, trying to block out the screams.

And yet, she reminded herself, good things had

happened in the amusement park too. She envisioned the photo of her and Tyler on the roller coaster, now stuck on Pepper's refrigerator. It was also where they'd been when Tyler had wished that Eden would know how special she was.

That memory burned inside her like a fire's ember. When she focused on it, the fire gained strength. It soothed her soul and melted her panic away.

She peered over her shoulder. "Okay. We should be fine."

"Phew!" said Melodie. "Gosh, that was scary!"

"You're telling me," said Eden.

"Are you sure it was them?"

"Definitely. One of Brightly's top people was talking to a group of men about finding me. They've already staked out the pyramid." She shook her head. "I should have known not to go near it."

"They're really desperate to find you," said Melodie in awe.

"No kidding." It was alarming to think about. It also reminded her how hard it was going to be to get the lamp out of Brightly Tech. "We've got to get to that Kiwi store." She looked at Melodie. "Are you sure you don't want to go home?"

"No way." Melodie's grin shone radiantly under her bright orange wig. "Even if I'm grounded till I'm twenty, it'll be worth it. This is the best day of my life."

Fourteen

The Champs-Élysées was a very wide street, lined with trees on both sides. As the girls strolled along the pedestrian-covered gray stone sidewalk, they passed large stores, multiplex movie theaters, and cafés with outdoor tables where people drank big glasses of wine or tiny cups of coffee.

Once again, Eden was struck by the contrast to New York. The buildings here were softer and lighter than Manhattan's skyscrapers, in shades of cream and rosy white. You could tell they'd been here longer, and that they were created to be looked at and enjoyed.

Along the way, Melodie asked a gray-haired gentleman in a lavender suit and top hat if she could take his photo for her blog. He agreed, and posed stoically for a few photographs. Eden made sure to stay out of the frame.

"Hey, she's got a nice outfit on," Eden said, pointing out a woman in a green silk blouse and black slacks.

"Eden," Melodie said admonishingly, "come on. She looks like a mannequin at a department store." Her eyes lit upon something ahead. "Now *they* have style."

About thirty yards ahead, two women were walking in their direction. One wore a loose, short-sleeved dress in maroon, and on her head was a tan hat with a wide brim. Her hair was long, limp, and colored a dull shade of turquoise. The other woman wore a red-and-blue-plaid blazer with black leather shorts. Her complexion was caramel-colored, and her hair was cut so short that she had almost none at all.

Eden was so focused on their clothes that she almost didn't look at their faces. When she did, she realized that she knew these women.

Their names were Monroe and Athena, and they were genie alumni who happened to be key members of Electra.

"Let's talk to them," said Melodie, striding forward.

Frantically, Eden turned to her left and saw a store with sportswear in the window. Quick as she could, she darted through the door and ducked behind a manne-quin decked out in tennis gear.

Peering around the mannequin, she watched Melodie approach the Electric. She introduced herself and indicated her camera, but the women barely even slowed their pace. Melodie trotted alongside them as she continued her explanation, but Monroe and Athena didn't even acknowledge her.

Eden's heart was pounding, and she was squeezing her fists so tight that her fingernails cut a row of curved impressions into her palms. She couldn't believe it. Paris had a population of more than two million people. How did she keep running into the ones she most needed to avoid?

Of course, Eden knew Electra was based here. Sylvana had tried to lure her here with beguiling descriptions of Paris's beauty and glamour. But Eden had gotten the impression that most of the Electric lived in other parts of the world, searching for the lamp in every corner they could cover.

She sincerely hoped that Monroe and Athena being here didn't have anything to do with her.

Finally, Melodie gave up. Wistfully she watched the Electric walk away, lifting her camera to snap a consolation shot from behind. Then she put down her camera and looked around in confusion. She was searching for Eden, of course.

Eden took a breath to regain her composure. Even though she was in disguise, she had to stay on high alert. Monroe and Athena might not have been fooled by a wig and a school uniform. Maybe no one would be, if they were looking hard enough.

Melodie spotted her through the window, and her face relaxed with relief. Eden waved and came out of the store.

"There you are!" Melodie exclaimed. "Why'd you run off?"

"I don't think I should get up close and personal with people." *These people in particular,* she thought.

"You're probably right," Melodie agreed. "Well, they blew me off anyway. They weren't nice at all." Her expression went a little dreamy. "But they were cool. So, so cool."

To Eden's relief, the Kiwi store was only a little farther. The façade was clear glass, so you could see straight through to the interior. Inside, everything was either silver or lime green: the floor, the walls, the long display tables, and the computers that sat on them. Shoppers swarmed the computers on display. The thought of being around so many people made Eden wary, but she wasn't going to back out now that they'd made it here.

Melodie went to a free computer and waved her over. "I'll log in to my account," she said quietly. "Then I'll be the lookout while you use it."

Once Eden had taken her place in front of the computer, it took no time to find the profile for Quincy Abbott. She started a message.

It's the kid from the street where you live, she wrote first.

That would let Pepper know it was her, but if Brightly, Jane, or anyone else from Brightly were to check Quincy Abbott's incoming messages, they'd assume the message was from Melodie.

But where should she say to meet her?

Eden closed her eyes and ran through a mental catalogue of the places she'd seen in Paris. Suddenly it hit her.

Tonight I'll be at the place named for the person who showed you the second part of your destiny.

Pepper would know that meant Shakespeare and Company, but no one at Brightly Tech would guess it. And Eden knew exactly how to get there.

She was counting on Pepper checking her messages, but Eden was pretty sure that she would. Brightly's announcement was all over the news in Paris, so Pepper would probably see it in the airport when she landed and wonder what was going on.

Eden logged out of Melodie's account and surveyed the store. No one was paying attention to her. Melodie gave her a thumbs-up.

Time for research.

First, she did a search for David Brightly and found a short bio about him. It said that he'd grown up in a tiny town in Kentucky. His father was a miner who regularly gambled away his earnings.

And probably lied about it, Eden thought.

David had started working to support his family when he was fourteen. In high school he won a full scholarship to Stanford University and studied there for one year, but then he dropped out and started Brightly Tech at the age of nineteen.

Eden bit her lip and thought. Brightly's upbringing probably would have caused his trust issues. And because he'd grown up poor, it made sense that he was so proud of having built his own company.

But how did Jane come into play?

Eden searched for Jane Johnston. Immediately she found an article dated four years earlier announcing that Jane had been named vice president of Brightly Tech. Apparently the hire had been a surprise for many, because she hadn't worked for the company previously.

"I've known Ms. Johnston for several years, and I have full confidence in her abilities," read a quote from Brightly in the article. *"Brightly Tech will benefit greatly from her leadership."*

Eden went back and looked at the other search results. The next one that caught her eye was a piece on a news Web site. The title was: WHO IS JANE JOHNSTON? THE MYSTERY BEHIND BRIGHTLY'S NEW HIRE.

Eden clicked it and started to read.

Last week, Brightly Tech head honcho David Brightly stunned the tech world with the announcement of his new vice president: a newcomer named Jane Johnston. Although Ms. Johnston allegedly has a background in computer science, attempts to verify her past employment, education, and even her birth have been fruitless.

"Hey," Melodie said from next to Eden. "That's Papa's story."

Eden turned to her in confusion. "What?"

Melodie pointed to the story's byline. "Christopher Laurent. That's Papa."

"You're kidding." Eden had nearly forgotten that Melodie's parents were journalists. "Do you think—"

"Mademoiselle." A salesperson in silver had sidled up to Eden. "Are you interested in buying this computer?"

Startled, Eden looked up at her. "I'm . . . not sure yet. I was testing it out."

The woman glared and tapped the lime-green watch on her wrist. "You've been testing it out for quite some time."

"Is there a time limit?" Melodie piped up defiantly. "I haven't seen a sign about a time limit."

The woman eyed them suspiciously. "Are your parents here?"

Melodie turned up her nose. "That's none of your business."

The woman's nostrils flared.

"Let's get out of here," Eden whispered. Causing a

scene wasn't going to help anything. She closed out of the Internet and took Melodie by the arm. *"Merci, au revoir!"* she said to the huffy saleslady as they left.

"I can't stand people like that," Melodie grumbled as they emerged back onto the Champs-Élysées.

"I know. But at least I got some information." Eden adjusted her beret.

"Why do you need to learn about your uncle's vice president?"

"I'm trying to understand their relationship," Eden explained. "From what I can tell, she's the only person who has any influence on him."

"Are you thinking you could get her to help you?"

"I doubt there's any chance of that," Eden said. "I just want to know more. It's hard to explain."

"Too bad we can't ask my dad," said Melodie. "It sounds like he wanted to know more about her too—and he would have done tons of research for that article. He probably knows way more than what was printed."

"Would he have notes?" Eden asked. "Maybe he would have kept them somewhere."

"Well, sure. In his office at the university." Melodie's eyes lit up with that mischievous glow. "Let's go find them!"

"Could we?" Eden asked excitedly.

"Oui! But first..."

She'd stopped next to a storefront that was decked

out in gold and sea-foam green. There was a glassed-in terrace with green and gold trimming, and green iron curled between the panes of glass. Gold letters spelled out the word LADURÉE.

But Melodie wasn't looking at the façade. Her eyes were on a glass display window. Inside it were rows of macarons, organized by their vibrant colors: hot pink, pistachio green, brown, yellow, purple, and creamy white. Eden couldn't even imagine what flavors some of them could be.

Macarons were one treat Goldie had never made in the lamp. In fact, Eden had only learned about them recently, in New York—but she hadn't tried them yet. Seeing the display, she was overcome by a strong urge to change that.

"Maybe we should stop here first," Melodie said. "For sustenance."

"Good idea," Eden agreed.

They sat at a table on the terrace and ordered an assortment of macarons. From the first bite, Eden was in love. They were light, fluffy, and delicious.

After trying a few different flavors, she bit into a yellow one and closed her eyes in rapture. "I know I keep changing my mind," she said, "but now it's officially official. Lemon is my favorite."

"But you haven't tried hazelnut yet!" Melodie pushed a light-brown one toward her.

Eden grinned and accepted it. "All right, let's get down to business. How are we going to find those notes?"

"Papa's office isn't far from my apartment." Melodie picked up a pink macaron. "So we'll have to keep an eye out for him and Maman. But I seriously doubt they'll be out looking for me. They're more likely to be sitting at home, plotting my punishment."

"Close to your apartment," Eden said. "Does that mean it's close to the library?"

"Well, it is part of the university too. But it's a few blocks away." She pushed some of the wig's fiery-orange fibers out of her face. "Do you think they'd still be waiting for you at the library?"

"I don't know," Eden said. "Will it be hard for us to get into the building?"

Melodie shrugged. "I don't think so. The building won't be locked. Papa's colleagues know me, so if any of them are around, I'll say I'm picking something up for him."

"Do you think it's safe for me to go with you?"

Suddenly, Melodie's face went pale. "Oh no. Oh no. Oh no."

"Okay..." Eden said uncertainly. "I'll wait outside or something."

"It's too late."

"Too late?"

But Melodie wasn't talking about their trip to the office anymore. Instead, she was staring at something behind Eden. "She saw me," she uttered dramatically.

"*Who?*" Eden whipped around to see. Standing on the sidewalk outside was a girl who appeared to be in her late teens. Her face looked like Melodie's, but her hair was long, and she wore a sensible black linen dress and flats. Her arms were crossed, and she was glaring at Melodie.

"Camille!" Melodie whispered.

"Who's Camille?" The girl was heading for the door to Ladurée.

"My sister." Melodie pulled a few bills from her wallet and tossed them on the table. "Quick, let's go."

"You have a sister?"

"*Oui.* She's in university."

"Melodie!" Camille stormed across the terrace. "What do you think you're doing? You're grounded! You should be at home!"

Eden looked around nervously. People at the tables around them were staring.

"We're leaving!" Melodie's chair scraped the ground as she jumped up from the table. Eden stood up too. "Please don't tell Maman and Papa!"

"Yeah, right! They're going crazy worrying about you!" Camille scrutinized her. "What are you wearing?"

"Nothing," Melodie said defiantly.

Camille ripped the orange wig off her head, exposing the brown hair underneath. Then she reached out and yanked Melodie's nose ring right off her nostril.

"*Ow,*" Melodie howled.

"Oh, stop. It's a clip-on, it doesn't hurt! You know Maman hates it when you wear that."

Eden was relieved to know that Camille hadn't ripped Melodie's skin. But she also knew it wouldn't be smart to stick around while their sisterly squabble unfolded.

Camille's gaze landed on Eden. "Who are *you*?" she demanded.

"I—ah—" Eden stammered.

Camille reached toward Eden's brown bob. "Are you wearing a wig too?"

Eden ducked to dodge her hand, and Camille's eyes flared. "I'm calling Papa right now!" she announced.

Eden backed toward the door. "I think I should leave," she said.

"That's probably best," Melodie murmured.

Camille squinted at Eden. "Wait a second. You look familiar. Do I know you?"

"Run!" Melodie yelled.

And Eden did.

Fifteen

Eden tore down the Champs-Élysées, shouting *"Excusez-moi!"* and *"Désolée!"* as she sideswiped other pedestrians. She veered a sharp right at the first corner she came to and jetted toward the river.

Along the way, she glanced at a clock. It was 5:28 P.M. Three and a half hours to go.

She hoped that Melodie wasn't actually going to be grounded until she was twenty. She really had saved Eden. Without her guidance and the disguise, Eden would have been caught straightaway.

It was too bad they hadn't made it to her dad's office. Eden was dying to learn more of the story behind Jane and Brightly. But for now, all that mattered was making it to her meeting with Pepper.

She crossed a bridge to the Seine's south bank, then followed a set of stairs down to the water's level. To get to Shakespeare and Company, she just needed to follow the river all the way back there.

It was very important to get there promptly at nine, because if Pepper arrived and Eden wasn't there, Pepper might think she'd misinterpreted the message—or, worse, assume Eden had been caught. But it wouldn't take three and a half hours to walk there—and it wouldn't be smart to get there early and hang around. All the close calls had shown Eden that being around people was too risky. Her best bet now would be to find a hiding place and wait out the next few hours.

Down here, there were far fewer people; she'd only passed a handful of joggers and passersby. She paused under a bridge and sat against the cool concrete that curved under it. Maybe this was as good a hiding place as any. She leaned back and closed her eyes, and fatigue came crashing down on her. It was crazy to think she hadn't slept since the night before Tra La La Karaoke.

As her body relaxed, Eden's thoughts became calmer too. Even though she hadn't hatched a brilliant plan yet, she and Pepper would come up with one once they were together. Together they'd save the lamp and the masters, and then they'd go back to New York. They could still see *My Fair Lady*. Life would be better than ever....

"*Excusez-moi, mademoiselle.*"

Eden blinked, and discovered that her eyes were

heavy with sleep. She must have drifted off. The sky had grown dark, so she pulled off her sunglasses.

The man standing over her was stout and rosy-cheeked, and he wore a navy uniform with a patch on the chest. On the patch was the word POLICE.

"Shouldn't you be at home?" he asked gruffly.

"I'm just on my way there," she said, standing up. Her arms and legs were stiff and achy.

"I should hope so. A nice girl like you shouldn't be sleeping here." The man's expression was skeptical. "What's your name?"

Eden swallowed. "Uh . . . Marie."

"And do you attend the École Active Bilingue Jeannine Manuel?"

Eden thought about the best way to answer. "How did you know?" she asked at last.

"You're wearing their uniform."

She forced a smile. *"Mais oui,"* she said, as if she'd only been joking around.

"Then you must know my daughter, Nathalie Sauveterre."

"Who doesn't? She's a wonderful girl." Eden cleared her throat. "Well, I've got to be going." She started to walk away.

"Wait a moment!" The policeman looked Eden over. "I'm sure I've seen you before. Have you been to our house?"

"Non," she said firmly.

He shifted his weight. "You should be careful," he said. "A girl your age was just kidnapped."

Eden tried to seem nonchalant. "Oh, really?"

"Oui! The daughter of David Brightly! You know, from Brightly Tech." He held up his phone to show the logo on the back.

Eden swallowed. "That's horrible."

"C'est tragique!" he exclaimed. "Kidnapping a young girl! I can't imagine it. But the entire police force of Paris is searching for this girl." He waggled his finger passionately. "We will find her, I promise you that."

"I've got to get home," Eden said weakly.

"Why don't I escort you?" the policeman asked.

"No! Thanks, but no thanks. I'll be fine."

"I insist!" The policeman dipped in a little bow. "It is my duty. Besides, you're a friend of Nathalie. Tell me, where is your home?"

Desperately, Eden tried to think of a story to tell him. But she'd been telling lies all day, and she was fresh out of them.

"Your home," the policeman repeated. "Where is it?"

Eden shivered. When had it gotten so chilly? She had no idea how long she'd slept.

"What time is it?" she asked.

He checked his watch. "Eight fifty-six."

Four minutes until nine! Pepper would nearly be there!

"Almost your bedtime, I'd expect."

"I really do have to go!" Eden exclaimed.

"I told you, I'll drive you. I won't take no for an answer."

It seemed he really wouldn't, which meant she didn't have much of a choice. Plus, even if she were to take off this instant and run the whole way, she wouldn't make it in time anyway. By the time she got there, Pepper might be gone.

Eden took a deep breath. "Can you take me to Shakespeare and Company?" she asked. "I'm supposed to meet my mother there."

The policeman raised an eyebrow. "Late-night book shopping?"

Eden shrugged.

"Very well," he said. "Let's go."

As the police car pulled up to the bookstore, Eden saw Pepper standing outside. She was wearing a jacket and a newsboy hat and looking around expectantly. When she saw the police car, her expression became wary.

"There she is!" Eden said. "Thanks for the ride!"

"Not so fast," said the policeman. He turned off the engine. "I need to have a word with her."

By now, Eden knew there was no point arguing with him.

Please play along, she implored Pepper silently. *We're so close.*

When Pepper saw Eden climb from the car, the joy on her face shone like a lantern's glow. The wig didn't throw her off for an instant.

They rushed toward each other and embraced. "Oh my goodness, kid," she said. "Am I glad to see you!"

"You're my mother, and my name is Marie," Eden whispered in her ear. When she pulled back, she saw confusion in Pepper's eyes—but it was quickly replaced by a keen look of understanding.

"Bonsoir," said the policeman as he approached.

Eden hoped with all her might that Pepper's French wasn't rusty.

"Bonsoir, monsieur," she said smoothly. Eden felt a rush of relief.

"Do you know that your daughter was sleeping under a bridge?"

Pepper gasped. "Marie!" she exclaimed. "What were you thinking?"

"Sorry, Maman," Eden said meekly.

"We are going to have a serious discussion when we get home," Pepper assured the policeman.

"I should hope so," he said. "Did you hear about the

girl who was kidnapped last night? The daughter of David Brightly."

"I did hear," Pepper said, betraying nothing. "How *awful*."

"She's the same age as Marie and my daughter Nathalie, who's in her class. But don't worry. We will find her!" For someone so clueless, he sure was enthusiastic.

"Marie and I should get home," Pepper said. "Thank you for bringing her to me."

"You're welcome," he replied. "Can I drive you?"

"*Non, merci*. Our car is right here." Pepper indicated a black sedan parked in front of the police car.

"*Très bien*. Have a good night—and a safe one!"

"*Merci!*" they said. Pepper blew him a kiss.

"Marie, I'll tell Nathalie you said hello!" the policeman called.

As he drove away, Eden let out a huge sigh of relief. "Sorry about that," she said. "You were incredible."

"Hey, we got through it," Pepper said, hugging her again. "Gosh, I'm so glad you're okay."

"And I'm so happy you're *here*!" Eden said.

"Listen," Pepper said. "I've got to tell you something. I'm not here alone."

Eden pulled back. "Not alone? What do you mean?"

Just then, the dark-tinted back window of the sedan

rolled down. When Eden saw the person on the other side of it, her jaw dropped in disbelief. She was looking at someone she'd believed—and hoped—she'd never see again.

"What is *she* doing here?" Eden cried.

Sixteen

"Hello to you too," said Bola dryly. "And you're welcome, for putting my life on hold once again to come clean up your mess."

Eden glared at her. In San Diego, the sharp-tongued leader of the Loyal alumni had bullied and intimidated her. She'd even utilized the magical powers of another genie alum to give Eden the most terrifying experience of her life. Eden knew she'd done it all to protect the lamp and its masters—but still, she couldn't help disliking Bola.

Why on Earth had Pepper brought her here? Eden hadn't even thought they were friends.

"Can we go?" Bola snapped. "Or are we going to sit here and wait for the rest of the Paris police force to show up?"

Pepper put an arm around Eden and steered her to

the car. As they climbed in, Bola scooted over so Eden was sandwiched between the two of them.

"To Montmartre," Bola said to the driver in French. "The address I gave you." She slid the partition closed and sat back.

"Montmartre?" Eden asked. "Why there?"

Lessons in Parisian geography had taught her that Montmartre was an area perched across a large hill in the north part of the city. Through the years, it had come to be known as a haven for artists. Some of its esteemed residents had been Claude Monet, Pablo Picasso, Salvador Dalí, and Vincent van Gogh (who'd apparently been a nightmare during his granting with a genie named Bambi). The neighborhood had a reputation for being colorful and offbeat.

"A Loyal alum named Delta owns a house up here," Pepper said as the car began to climb the steep roads. "We're going to stay with her—at least for tonight."

Eden remembered Delta, a genie who'd been in the lamp from AD 211 to 309. In her portrait in the genie course guide, Delta had a small heart-shaped face and a gap between her two front teeth. But Eden didn't know anything about her except what she'd learned in Lamp History. She didn't think the masters exchanged messages with her.

"Let's get down to it," Bola said impatiently in her

crisp British accent. She brushed her bloodred dreadlocks behind her shoulder. In San Diego she'd worn her hair in a bun high on her head, but now it hung long and loose. "Pepper filled me in on what happened after San Diego—how you're living on Earth now, et cetera. Everything up until the night when you were summoned. This morning you messaged her asking for help, and then, shortly after, David Brightly issued a statement claiming that you're his kidnapped daughter. And tonight, you were escorted to us by a policeman. What *happened*?"

Eden told her story as swiftly as possible, starting with Brightly Tech, then moving on to Melodie, the Sorbonne Library, the Louvre, what she'd learned about Jane Johnston, the close call with Camille, and the policeman.

As she spoke, Bola's face twisted up tighter and tighter, as if she had to physically restrain her words from breaking through. Finally, when Eden finished, they erupted.

"This is a *dire* emergency!" she burst out.

"Bola," Pepper said, "let's stay calm."

"Calm?! We're in a veritable state of disaster!"

Pepper eyed her warily. "True, there is a lot to figure out—but at least Eden is safe."

"Is she?" Bola barked.

"For now I am," said Eden.

"For now—exactly! And what about the lamp? You left it there, with that horrible mortal!"

"What else was I supposed to do?" Eden cried. "I told you, I couldn't take it!"

"I'm sure you could have thought of *something*!"

"Like *what*?"

Bola eyed her menacingly. "I can't believe you'd let something like this happen to your masters. After they gave you exactly what you wanted! They changed the rules for you!"

"Excuse me." Pepper leaned across the car's backseat to get a good look at Bola. "I am Eden's guardian, and no one's going to get away with talking to her like that. Not while I'm around."

Eden tried to hide her glee. Clearly, the masters knew what they were doing when they chose Pepper as her earthly guardian.

"Now listen to me," Pepper went on. "I asked for your help because Xavier and Goldie advised me to. But if you're going to antagonize Eden, you can go *right* back where you came from." Pepper paused for emphasis. "Anyway, Eden didn't *let* anything happen. There's nothing she could have done to prevent this. And she's been through a lot in the past twenty-four hours. Now, you can help us figure out how to fix this, or this gentleman can drive you right back to the airport. What's it going to be?"

Bola exhaled slowly and lowered her eyes. "You're right. I apologize." Eden could barely believe it. As shocking as Pepper's speech had been, seeing Bola back down was even more unreal.

"You're going to help?"

"Yes."

"Then you need to work with us, not against us."

The car's partition slid open, and the driver peered through at them.

"Is this it?" he asked in French.

They hadn't even noticed that the car had stopped. All three of them turned toward the window. Outside it were three buildings, snug up against each other with no space between, as if huddled together for warmth.

Two of them were well-kept and friendly-looking. The one on the left was cream-colored with green shutters, and the one on the right was pale blue with gray shutters. Each had five rows of four windows across.

But the building in the middle was different.

It only had three rows of windows, so it was dwarfed by its two taller neighbors. It looked like perhaps it had once been white, but time had turned it a muddy light brown. And it was covered with brittle, dead-looking ivy.

Eden shuddered. It reminded her of stories she'd read about haunted houses.

"Oh dear," Bola murmured. "She's let it get even worse than the last time I saw it. Yes, just here," she said to the driver. She slipped some cash through the partition, and he got out to help Bola and Pepper unload their suitcases from the trunk.

Eden stood staring at the house uneasily. "This is where she lives?"

"For the past hundred and fifty years," Bola said through her teeth. "Let's get inside." She strode up to the door, dragging a chic black alligator-skin suitcase on wheels, and struck the brass knocker against the door.

Behind her, Pepper took Eden's hand.

Bola hit the knocker again, but still, no one came. Montmartre was silent—at least, outside of Delta's door. Inside, there seemed to be some sort of commotion.

"Are those *birds*?" Eden asked.

Grumbling, Bola took the doorknob and pushed the door open.

If the outside of the house was run-down, the inside was downright dilapidated. Crimson-and-gold wallpaper was peeling off the walls. There were gaps between the floorboards. A smell of mothballs and mildew hung in the air. And something else . . .

"Ahhh!" Pepper shrieked, ducking. There was the sound of flapping wings, and a gust of air.

"What was that?!" Eden cried.

The flapping thing flew in circles around them in a blur of gray.

"Frederick!" screamed a voice upstairs. There was the sound of quick footsteps as a woman ran down the worn red-carpet-covered stairs.

Delta would have been nearly ninety years old when she retired. (In the early days, genies' careers had lasted longer because fewer mortals populated the Earth, meaning the lamp was found less frequently.) She certainly didn't look that old now; her face lacked the deep lines of old age. Eden would guess that she'd wished to look middle-aged—perhaps somewhere around fifty. But she was gaunt and haggard, with wiry brown hair in the shape of a bird's nest. She wore a ratty pink terry-cloth bathrobe and slippers.

"Hello, hello, hello!" she called as she hit the bottom of the stairs. She crossed her arms and nodded. "Bola."

"Delta," Bola said. "Thank you for letting us drop in."

"And which of you is the resident genie?" There was a disconcerting gleam in Delta's eyes.

"I am." Eden stuck out a hand the way she'd learned to do when she met new people on Earth, but Delta ignored it.

"Are you wearing a wig?" she asked, staring unapologetically. Her eye sockets were enormous.

"Oh, yeah." Eden had almost forgotten she didn't

need it anymore. She slid the beret and the brown bob off her head, pulled the elastic out of her hair, and shook it out.

"My, my," Delta said. She grinned, and Eden saw that the gap between her front teeth was as wide as ever. "I can't wait to pick your brain."

"I'm Pepper," Pepper spoke up. "Pleased to meet you." Eden could tell that, despite the circumstances, she was trying her very best to be polite.

The gray thing whizzed by again.

"Frederick!" This time, Delta reached out and swiped it out of the air. She opened her cupped hands to reveal a tiny bird.

"Is that a zebra finch?" Eden asked. What had looked like a gray blur was actually the finch's striped white-and-black pattern. The orange color on its cheeks meant it was a male.

"Yes—very good." Delta rubbed the back of her index finger along the bird's side. "One of my boys. This one's a troublemaker. Oh, hello there." She was smiling at a random spot on the floor.

Bola cleared her throat. "Will we be staying upstairs?"

Delta seemed to rejoin them in reality. "Yes, yes. Come with me."

As the three of them followed her up the stairs, Pepper and Eden exchanged a wide-eyed look.

"I have two rooms for guests," Delta said, indicating them once they'd reached the second floor.

"Eden and I will take one," Pepper said. "You can have the other one, Bola."

"The pets and I live on the third floor." Delta pointed to another staircase. On this one, the carpet was worn away almost completely.

Eden shivered. She hoped there wouldn't be any need for her to go up there.

"Freshen up, and then come downstairs," Delta said. "Dinner will be served in ten minutes."

Eden was surprised, because she hadn't smelled anything cooking. Still, she was glad to hear there would be food. She followed Pepper into their bedroom.

Peeling wallpaper in a dull blue floral print covered the walls. In the center of the room was a saggy bed with a yellowy comforter. A scraggly teddy bear with creepy eyes slumped against the pillows, but Pepper immediately took it by the arm and tossed it off. She kneeled on the floor and opened her suitcase.

"Want to change?" she asked. "I brought some of your clothes."

But Eden couldn't pretend everything was normal. Something had been nagging at her for the past half hour.

"Pepper," she said, "why did you ask Bola to come?"

Pepper looked up from the suitcase.

"I thought that you and I could take care of this together. Now that Bola's involved, it changes everything," Eden continued.

Pepper got off the floor and sat cross-legged on the bed. The mattress gave a weird groan and sank down where she sat.

For the first time, Eden noticed how tired Pepper looked. Beneath her eyes were dark circles, and although Eden was sure nothing in the world could take away their sparkle, it definitely wasn't as bright as before.

"Eden," Pepper said, "last night when you didn't come back, I was terrified. I waited for hours. I tried messaging the masters, but my messages wouldn't go through. I knew something was very wrong." She swallowed. "Xavier and Goldie had told me that if something ever came up that they couldn't help with, I should get in touch with Bola. So I did."

"But now that Bola knows I'm living on Earth, everything's going to be different. Once we get the lamp back, I want it to be you and me again, back in New York." Eden fought to keep her voice from shaking. "Like it was."

"It *will* be," Pepper insisted. "But we can't do this alone. We need help." She took a breath. "Look, I know Bola isn't your favorite person. Frankly, she's not mine either." Pepper whispered this part, and made a funny face. "But she's going to help us."

"I guess so," said Eden reluctantly.

"Why don't you change your clothes, and then we'll see what Delta's made for dinner? Hopefully it'll be fresher than this house." Pepper stuck out her tongue.

As she changed into a T-shirt and cotton shorts in the bathroom, Eden hoped with all her might that Pepper was right.

Hopefully, Bola wasn't going to cause more harm than good.

Seventeen

If anything, Delta's dinner was a little *too* fresh. Once they'd sat around the table in the dining room downstairs, she served each of them what looked like a thick, raw hamburger patty topped with an egg yolk.

"Steak tartare," she said proudly. "A Parisian specialty. *Bon appétit!*"

Eden looked down at it dubiously. She liked steak, but she'd always eaten it cooked.

"I filled Delta in," Bola said. The raw meat didn't seem to bother her at all; she dug right in.

Eden poked the egg yolk with her fork. The yellow orb started to ooze onto the meat.

"The resident genie, living here on Earth. I never would have dreamed of this." When Delta grinned, the gap between her front teeth made her look like a jack-o'-lantern. Frederick and another zebra finch sat on her right shoulder, pecking at one another.

"Let's focus on the matter at hand," Bola said.

"The way I see it," Pepper said, "we've got to get the lamp back from Brightly's lab. We'll figure out how to remove the plasma shield; then Eden can make a request for reentry." Pepper seemed as hesitant as Eden about the tartare; she hadn't taken a bite yet either.

Eden felt an unexpected blast of warm air on her leg. She looked down but saw nothing. She scratched the spot with the heel of her other foot.

"So first, we plan an operation to get into Brightly's lab," Bola said. "Eden, what type of security do they have?"

"I'm not sure," Eden said, trying to remember. "But I'm guessing it's pretty advanced. Everything looked really high-tech, and they controlled things using electronic tablets. Like that magnetic force that kept me stuck in the chair." She smushed the tines of her fork into the tartare, making it flat and wide like a pancake.

"Well, we're not dealing with amateurs," Bola said. "Eden, stop playing with your food." Eden speared a tiny bit of meat and put it in her mouth. Actually, it wasn't bad.

"Are there Loyals whose powers can help us?" Pepper asked.

Eden got a surge of giddy curiosity. She'd always wanted to know this stuff. "Yeah! Do you guys know everyone's powers?"

Bola cleared her throat importantly and threw her shoulders back. "As you know, an alum's thousandth wish is secret unless she chooses to share it. However, many Loyal alumni have chosen to confide in me, in case any powers or skills they acquired might be useful for the cause."

"Tell me!" Eden said. "I want to know them all!"

Bola shot Eden a glare cold enough to cause frostbite. "I can't help thinking that sharing this information is *highly* inappropriate." She sighed. "However, I suppose it's necessary."

"So?" Pepper asked. "Who's going to help us? Are other Loyals on their way?"

"No. We don't need anyone who's not in this room," Bola said. "Which is for the best. I'd prefer for the other Loyals not to know what's going on. A few of them saw Brightly's announcement and have already contacted me, but I've told them the situation is under control."

"Why?" Eden asked. It seemed strange, considering Bola had called them all to San Diego a couple weeks earlier.

"They'd go into an uproar if they knew the entrance to the lamp was blocked. And anyway, Xavier and Goldie didn't want everyone to know that Eden's living on Earth. And I always respect their wishes." She eyed the others around the table. "So. This remains between us four."

"But how will we do it?" Pepper asked, looking puzzled.

"Well, Delta will be crucial."

Eden looked at Delta. She seemed to have checked out of the conversation, and was letting the finches on her shoulder nibble from her fork. She might as well have been on another planet.

How was she going to be helpful? Next to Eden, Pepper looked doubtful too.

"When Delta retired," Bola said, "she wished for the ability to make things invisible."

"Only one thing at a time," Delta said, without taking her eyes off the finches. Apparently she was listening after all.

"Really?" Eden asked. "What do you use that for?"

Delta turned from the birds to a spot on the floor next to Eden. Suddenly, a high-pitched bark pierced the air. Eden screamed and leapt up from her chair. Below her was a golden retriever puppy.

"That's Trevor. He wants your tartare. Better eat up," Delta said.

Pepper had leapt up too. "How long has he been there?" she sputtered.

"Since we sat down," Delta said calmly.

"But I didn't hear him either!" Eden exclaimed.

"That's because I don't just make things invisible to

the eyes. I make them invisible to the ear as well," Delta said. "You can feel them and smell them, but you can't see or hear them."

"I thought I felt something breathing on me down there." Eden leaned down and scratched Trevor behind the ears. Now that he was visible, she could see how adorable he was.

"Have *you* been able to see him?" Pepper asked.

"Of course." Delta clapped her hands, and Trevor came bounding over.

"I figured you had something hiding in here," Bola muttered.

Eden and Pepper sat down again. "So you're thinking if we can get Delta into the lab, she can make the lamp invisible and smuggle it out?" Pepper asked.

"Something along those lines," Bola said.

"You won't be able to smuggle it out with that plasma shield protecting it," Eden said. "I know we're all immortal, but that pain was insane. We'll have to figure out how to remove the plasma shield in the lab."

Bola cleared her throat. "That won't be a problem."

"What do you mean?" Eden asked.

Bola sighed. "I don't like sharing this. Again, I must request that you keep this information between us."

"*What?*"

Bola cleared her throat. "I don't feel pain," she said.

Eden raised her eyebrows. Beside her, Pepper's eyes widened.

"Like, at all?"

"No," Bola said. "It was part of my thousandth wish." Eden had never seen her as uncomfortable as she seemed now.

"Whoa," Pepper said softly.

"Like, emotional pain too?" Eden asked. That would explain a few things.

"*No!*" Bola scoffed. "Of course I feel pain *emotionally*. Do you think I'm a monster?"

Eden zipped her mouth shut.

"The point is, I won't have a problem removing the lamp from the plasma shield. Now can we move on?" As much as Bola liked taking charge, she sure didn't seem to like talking about herself.

"Okay," said Pepper, shrugging. "Then it sounds like we have a plan. Or the start of one, at least. When is this going to happen?"

"As soon as possible," Bola said. "Eden, we can find the location of Brightly Tech online. Can you tell us how to get to the lab once we're inside the building?"

"Negative."

Bola threw back her head in exasperation.

"Sorry! I was in those two rooms the whole time, so I never saw any other part of the building. I know it was high up, because I fell a really long way when I jumped. But I couldn't tell you what level we were on, or how to get there. I was a little traumatized, if you know what I mean."

"Not a worry," Pepper said cheerfully. "We'll figure it out once we get there."

"Hmmmm." Delta's voice wavered between pitches in a spooky melody. "I don't think so." She shook her head emphatically, her bird's nest of hair flying out in all directions. "Not if we don't know where to go."

"Well, what's the alternative?" Bola asked.

Delta held her plate below the table so Trevor could lick the remains.

"I could go to Brightly Tech tomorrow morning," Pepper said. "I'll feed them a false tip about Eden's whereabouts! Trust me, I know how to play a role. Then, I can check out the building's layout from inside."

"You can't show your face in there, Pepper," Bola snapped. "We're dealing with the world's most powerful tech mogul."

"So?"

"You're all over social media!" Bola rolled her eyes. "I don't understand how no one's figured out you've had ten different names."

"Seven." Pepper crossed her arms and pouted.

"I'm also too visible," Bola said. "God knows what I

could be traced to. I've held a few prominent positions in my day."

Eden made a mental note to ask Pepper about that later.

"You think he could connect you to those?" she asked.

"Of course. The way they tracked Eden today proves he can access anything." She eyed them one by one. "By the way, I hope you've turned your cell phones off. Obviously, it's not safe for us to use them until we've retrieved the lamp."

"Oh, right. Good point," said Pepper. She pulled hers out of her pocket and powered it off. "I brought Eden's here, too, but it hasn't been on since I left New York."

"I've never had a cell phone," Delta said.

Bola's eyes rested on Delta. "That's true. You could go to Brightly Tech, Delta."

Delta twitched her nose and blinked rapidly.

"Why could Delta go?" Eden asked.

"She's completely off the grid," Bola said. "I had to call the house's landline to reach her today."

"I've never even touched a computer," said Delta, wide-eyed.

"Me neither, until this morning," Eden reassured her.

"Okay then," Pepper said. "Delta will go tomorrow morning, and try to find the best way to get to that lab."

"Wait," Eden said. "Delta, can you make *people* disappear?"

She nodded rapidly. "Yes, of course."

Eden's toes tapped excitedly on the floor. "Why don't I go with her? If Delta makes me disappear, I can sneak around and learn more."

"Absolutely not," Bola said. "You're the one they're all searching for."

"But they wouldn't be able to see me! Only Delta could."

"No. If anyone's going to go invisible and do recon, it should be me or Pepper."

"But you weren't there before," Eden said. "I was! Like I said, I can't tell you how to get to the place where they had me—but if I go there, I'm sure I can find it."

"Bola," Pepper said, "she has a point. You and I wouldn't be as effective. We wouldn't know what we were looking for."

"But look at her track record," Bola said, gesturing toward Eden. "She's shown herself to be far from responsible. And besides that, she's a *child*."

"What did I tell you?" That defiant spark was back in Pepper's eyes. "Don't condescend to Eden. We're all working together on this."

"Bola, look," Eden said. She leaned forward and gazed right into Bola's ice-cold eyes. "I may feel pain, but I'm still immortal. No one can *really* hurt me. The worst they could do is trap me again—but they can't even do that if they can't see or hear me." She swallowed. "I'll be just like a ghost. Right, Delta?"

"Exactly," Delta whispered. Her eyes were enormous as she nodded. "You'll be a ghost."

"I don't like the idea of sending her back in there either," Pepper said. "Of *course* I don't. But I do trust Eden. She's a smart kid, and this is a smart idea."

Eden's cheeks warmed with pride.

Bola looked from Pepper to Delta, and then, finally, at Eden. She sighed dramatically. "Fine. I can't believe I'm agreeing to this."

"Trust me," Eden said. "I won't let you down."

Trevor barked.

"Trevor agrees," said Delta. And even Bola had to laugh.

Eighteen

A few arrondissements away, the inner circle of Electra assembled at headquarters.

They met in the third-floor executive boardroom. Eight white leather office chairs surrounded a polished walnut table. Remote-controlled wood-paneled walls could slide open to expose an exquisite view of Avenue Montaigne through full-length windows; but tonight, they were closed. Real Electra meetings—not the ones about art and auctions, but the ones about the lamp—were rare, shrouded in secrecy, and always, like this one, held at night.

Normally, gossip and laughter preceded board meetings, but tonight only nervous whispers floated through the air.

"Ladies," Sylvana said, "let us begin."

She was sitting at the table's head, of course, wearing a sleek black pantsuit and killer pumps. Her lengths of gold hair were wound into a no-nonsense bun, and burgundy lipstick made even her mouth look dangerous.

Violet was sitting on her right side. She'd made sure to be the first one in the room so she could claim the coveted seat.

"Thank you all for making your way here on such short notice," Sylvana said. "Though I wouldn't expect anything less from my inner circle." Indeed, almost all of the key Electric were here: Violet, Athena, Kingsley, Monroe, Julianna, and Heloise. Sylvana had sent them a tersely worded e-mail, informing them that their presence was required. Only Zoe was missing; she'd stayed in San Diego to keep an eye on the Rockwell family.

Heloise was the newest addition to this group. She sat across from Violet, on Sylvana's other side. Heloise had been a member of Electra in the early 1900s, but she'd left after a disagreement with Sylvana that Violet didn't know much about. About a year ago she'd come crawling back, and had quickly managed to weasel her way into the inner circle.

Heloise was very tall, with thick but well-groomed eyebrows and cheekbones so prominent, their shadows were slashes on her cheeks. Her silky hair was shoulder-length, and she always dressed like she'd just stepped off a runway.

Sylvana eyed them importantly. "Everyone knows

why we've gathered. An American businessman by the name of David Brightly has released a statement claiming that his daughter has been kidnapped. That 'daughter' is our very own Eden."

The women nodded, carefully concealing their reactions.

"As you all know, several weeks ago, we came closer to achieving our mission than ever before. Since I founded Electra in 1757, we've never been so close to acquiring the lamp." Sylvana gripped the table, and her nostrils flared. "Unfortunately, *Eden*"—she said the name like it was a disease—"took us for fools. Not Xavier or Goldie, but a naïve, powerless baby genie. A twelve-year-old. A *child*!"

Next to Violet, Monroe was scowling, as usual. Monroe's clothes hung off her gaunt frame; her hair, currently turquoise, hung straight and limp around her face; her complexion was cadaver-pale, and her eyes looked half-dead. Everyone knew that part of her thousandth wish was to not need sleep. Maybe it was time-effective, but it made her seem more phantom than human. And really, what was the point of saving time when you had eternity?

"Clearly," Sylvana went on, "Brightly is a thwarted wisher. He certainly isn't the first. But if we play this right, we'll make him the last."

"Do you have a plan, Sylvana?" Kingsley piped up.

Kingsley had the lovely face and soft blond curls of an angel, but she was as cruel and cunning as they come.

Sylvana smiled. "Of course I have a plan."

A familiar blend of admiration and envy stirred in Violet. Without exception, even when a situation looked wrong from every angle, Sylvana always had a plan.

"But first, I have an announcement to make. As you all know, every thirty years I appoint a new CEO, so as not to arouse the suspicion of mortals."

Violet stiffened as adrenaline shot through her veins.

From the time Electra was founded, its alumni members had roamed the world, supposedly seeking treasures for the auction house to acquire and sell. Of course, they were actually searching for the lamp—but the mortal employees who handled day-to-day operations didn't know that. By the late 1800s, Electra was thriving, and Sylvana decided she needed a genie alum to help her run the company. So Athena, the first alum to join Electra, became its very first CEO. After thirty years, Athena returned to obscurity and Monroe replaced her. The position was given to Kingsley next, and then Julianna. Violet wanted it more than anything in the world.

"Julianna has been CEO for the last thirty years," Sylvana continued, "and she's done the job well. But tomorrow morning, she will leave for a well-earned sabbatical in Japan. Tonight, someone will take her place."

Blood rushed to Violet's head. This time, it *had* to be her. Now, more than ever before, she'd proven herself. *She'd* found Eden with the lamp. She'd spied on Eden at the Rockwells' apartment. She'd enticed Bill Rockwell to the amusement park. It wasn't *her* fault things had gone awry from there. She'd done everything right—hadn't she?

"Our new CEO has shown herself to be crucial to Electra," said Sylvana. "She's sharp, she's decisive, and she commands respect. Most importantly, she is single-mindedly devoted to our cause. Under her leadership, we *will* acquire the lamp."

Violet swallowed. This was it.

"Ladies, I present to you Electra's new CEO."

The chairs creaked softly as the women leaned forward on the polished walnut table.

"Heloise."

Violet had been struck by lightning a few times. (When you'd been on Earth for nearly twenty-five hundred years, these things happened now and then.) Being immortal, she was also un-injurable, so the lightning couldn't do any real damage—but it *hurt*.

When Heloise's name passed through Sylvana's lips, it hit Violet just like lightning.

With a start, she realized the room was applauding. Dazedly, she clapped a few times too.

Heloise rose from her white leather chair and air-kissed Sylvana on both cheeks. Sylvana whispered something in her ear, and Heloise laughed.

The burn of betrayal sizzled on Violet's skin.

"Now, for the plan," said Sylvana. "Essentially, we've got to make David Brightly our new best friend. Ladies, you know how this works. Tomorrow night we have the Paris Jewels auction. The crème de la crème of Paris will be there. Tomorrow morning, Heloise and I will pay a visit to Mr. Brightly and extend him a personal invitation."

No one questioned whether Brightly would want to show his face at an auction the day after announcing his daughter's disappearance. Mortals never said no to Sylvana.

"Once he's in my pocket, we'll talk about the lamp and see what he knows." Sylvana drummed her fingertips on the table. "And then our *real* work will begin."

Nineteen

The next morning, a chorus of chirping birds ensured that everyone in the Montmartre house was awake at dawn.

"How many birds does she *have*?" Eden moaned, turning on her side.

"Who knows," Pepper answered, sounding as sleepy as Eden felt. "Wanna go upstairs and find out?"

"Yeah, right."

Eden's sleep had been uneasy. The bed was squeaky and saggy, and mysterious noises came from every direction. It was impossible to know whether it was just the old house settling, or other animals—visible or otherwise.

And yet, those were small matters compared to the worrisome thoughts that had tormented Eden all night.

She'd been so quick to volunteer to accompany Delta to Brightly Tech. She didn't regret it, exactly, but lying in bed, she'd started to remember how she'd felt the night before. The unbelievable force that had kept her trapped in that awful chair. The sensation of needles being stabbed into her skin again and again. And worst of all, the feeling of being regarded as an experiment rather than a person.

She reminded herself that Delta's power was going to conceal her completely. That she was immortal. That she was brave. And that once they got the lamp back, she and Pepper would be free to return to New York.

She was still scared. But those reminders had helped.

A hard knock came at the door.

"Come in!" Pepper croaked.

Bola pulled the door open. She was already dressed in a black T-shirt, black jeans, and combat boots. Standing in the doorway with her hands on her hips, she looked like a shadowy superhero—or maybe a villain.

"Delta and I are going to the bakery to pick up food for breakfast." She didn't bother with a greeting—just launched right in, as if they were in the middle of a conversation. Eden supposed "rise and shine" wasn't Bola's style. "Get up, get dressed, and meet us downstairs."

"This *early*?" Eden moaned. Through the window, the sky was only just beginning to light up.

Bola shot her a glare. "As if we have time to waste," she snapped. And just like that, she was gone.

"Good morning to you too, sunshine," Pepper murmured.

Eden swung her feet onto the battered wood floor. Realistically, she wouldn't have been able to go back to sleep anyway.

"I'll shower first," she said to Pepper.

Over fruit and croissants, they cemented their plan. Bola would drive Delta's car, a boxy brown Renault from the 1980s. Pepper and Delta would ride along, as would Eden—though only Delta would be able to see her. She was going to make Eden invisible before they left the house.

They'd park the car around the corner from Brightly Tech. (Even though Eden had no idea where she'd run from the morning before, Bola had looked up the facility's location as soon as she and Pepper had landed in Paris and saw the news.) Delta would go inside and tell the receptionist that she had information about Eden. Hopefully she'd have to wait to speak to someone. While she did, Eden would see if she could find the lab where she'd seen the lamp.

"That's your one job today, Eden. Do you understand?" Bola said. "We want you in and out of there as quickly as possible. No messing around."

"Yeah, I understand. Pretty simple." Eden forced

herself not to roll her eyes. It was like Bola thought she was a little kid.

"All right," said Bola. "Let's get going. Eden, are you ready?"

Eden had just finished her croissant. She brushed the crumbs off her fingers and stood up. "Ready as I'll ever be."

"Delta?"

With no fuss or deliberation, Delta looked up and made eye contact with Eden.

Pepper shrieked. "I can't *believe* it!" With a stunned look on her face, she came right up to where Eden was standing—so close, Eden had to take a step back.

"Hey," she said, laughing.

"She can't hear you," Delta said. "You're already gone."

"I am?" Eden looked down at her body. Everything looked and felt completely normal. She could see her jeans on her lanky legs, and the sneakers on her feet. She could see her arms, her hands, her genie bracelet, and the end of her blond braid. Even her voice sounded normal.

"That's incredible!" Pepper hooted.

"I can see and hear you," Delta said. "But no one else can."

"What is she saying?" Pepper asked.

"Nothing much," Delta said absently.

Bola walked up and examined Eden—or, rather, the empty space they now saw instead of her. She nodded, satisfied.

"Very good," she said. "Let's go."

The lobby of Brightly Tech looked more like a normal office building than what Eden had seen upstairs. Rather than the harsh white, fluorescent-lighted space, there was gray marble floor, a waiting area with black leather settees, and a big black desk where two receptionists sat.

To the right and left of the receptionists were elevators. Employees arriving for work, holding briefcases and takeaway coffee cups, exchanged greetings with one another and filed onto the elevators to start the workday.

Once they'd entered through the revolving doors, Delta gave Eden one final nod, then approached the reception desk. Eden hung back, watching the employees. Ideally, she'd see one she recognized and follow him or her to the floor where she'd been. Even though she couldn't be seen or heard, she still had to use the elevator like everyone else.

She watched Delta speak to the receptionist, then sit on a settee. She still hadn't spotted anyone she recognized, but she'd have to get going anyway. She followed two women onto an elevator and flattened herself against the wall.

She examined the buttons. There were eight floors.

"I don't think anyone knew," said one of the women in French. She pressed the button for the fourth floor. "But are you surprised? I've been working here for three years, and I know nothing about him."

"But a *daughter*! That's a big thing to hide."

Eden stiffened. They were talking about *her*! She supposed it would be a popular topic in the office.

"Apparently she was his sister's daughter. I didn't even know he had a sister."

"He certainly knows how to protect his privacy."

The elevator hit the fourth floor and the women stepped off. Outside the elevator was a hallway with gray carpet on the floor, and normal wooden doors along the walls. Definitely not where Eden had been. Anyway, she was sure she'd been up higher than four stories.

Alone on the elevator, Eden pressed the button for the eighth floor. The elevator rose again.

The doors opened to a reception desk in front of a wooden wall. The receptionist seemed to be the gateway to whatever the floor held. This was more promising, at least. Eden stepped off the elevator.

The receptionist pushed up her glasses and frowned directly at Eden. For a moment Eden was afraid she'd somehow slipped out of the ghost state and become visible, but then she realized the receptionist was confused because the elevator had seemed to come up with no one in it.

In the wall behind the receptionist was a door made of the same chestnut-colored wood as the wall itself. Eden walked past the reception desk and up to the door. Carefully, she put out a hand to test the door's handle. Not surprisingly, it was locked—but to the left of the door frame was a sensor.

From behind the desk, Eden could see that the receptionist was reading a news Web site on her computer. Lying beside the keyboard was an ID card displaying the receptionist's name and photo.

Surely that ID would open the door. But picking it up right in front of the receptionist would attract her attention. Eden needed to create a distraction.

It was time to be a ghost.

On the other side of the desk was a wire-mesh cup filled with pens and pencils. Eden crept over and pushed it off the edge, so the cup crashed onto the floor and the pens spilled out. The receptionist cried out and stared in its direction. She stood up and went to examine the mess.

Quickly, Eden swept the ID card off the desk and held it to the sensor. To her delight, she heard a quiet click. This time she was able to push the handle down.

She tossed the ID back onto the desk, then opened the door, slipped through, and closed it softly behind her.

On the other side of the door was a large rectangular area with white carpet and walls of the same dark chestnut wood. Stretching across the middle was a giant fish tank. It was nearly twice as tall as she was, and even longer than it was tall. Inside were dozens of fish in colors like royal blue, shocking pink, and the fiery orange of Melodie's wig.

Eden moved forward, and discovered a glass door on the wall to her left. A gold plate mounted next to it read JEAN LUC MOREAU.

Jean Luc was the name of the man in the lab last night! That had to mean she was close.

Peering through the glass, Eden saw an immaculate office space with several bookshelves and a desk that faced floor-to-ceiling windows. It was empty, though— no Jean Luc in sight.

A little farther down was another glass door. This office was nearly identical, but the name on the plate beside it read DR. PATRICK EVANS. And after that, a third office: JANE JOHNSTON.

Apparently, the eighth floor was where Brightly's most valued employees did their office work. But what about their work in the lab? Where was it?

The door to Jane's office was the last one on the left side. Turning to the right, Eden walked beside the fish tank. There was an entire rainbow of them! So far on Earth, she hadn't had an opportunity to look at real, live fish, and she found herself captivated.

"How could I say no to ladies as lovely as yourselves?"

The sound of the familiar Southern drawl shook Eden out of her trance. She whipped around to see David Brightly emerging from a glass door on the right side of the room. On the gold plate beside it was his name.

Brightly was walking with a cane. The burn from the laser must have been serious.

And he wasn't alone. By his side was the head of Electra herself: Sylvana.

Eden's stomach did a backflip.

Of course, she'd known there was a possibility that the Electric would investigate why Brightly had reported her missing. But Sylvana and her underlings had no idea that Eden was living on Earth. They didn't know that the lamp's rules had changed, and that the bracelet no longer bound her the way it had every other genie. They probably thought Eden was back inside the lamp already, and that Brightly's search was futile.

Still, here they were. Clearly, Sylvana was following any lead she could get.

With Brightly and Sylvana was another woman whom Eden had never seen before. She was unusually tall, towering above Brightly and even making Sylvana look short. Her cheekbones were sharply pronounced, and her smooth, straight hair was shoulder-length. She wore a long black dress with a high neck. From the waist up, the fabric was covered with spiky gold pieces that threatened to puncture anyone who got too close.

"I can't say I know much about jewelry," Brightly said as they whisked by.

"We'll teach you," Sylvana cooed. As usual, she looked exquisite. She wore a turquoise wrap dress with nude-colored heels, and her honey-blond hair was long and full. The smell of roses wafted behind her.

Eden followed them. Wherever they were going, she was going too.

Of course, she'd come in with the intention of finding the lab. But she'd stumbled upon her two worst enemies convening—and she was invisible! It was the perfect opportunity to spy on them.

Besides, she thought, maybe she'd hear something that would reveal where the lamp was. Maybe she'd even get some insight on how to save it.

Brightly led them to the same door she'd entered through and held it open for the women. When he let go, Eden held it and sneaked out behind them.

"Marguerite, be a sweetheart and cancel my appointments this morning," Brightly instructed as he pressed the elevator button.

"But, Monsieur—" the receptionist stammered.

"And why don't you eat something? You don't look well, darlin'." Brightly's tone sounded sweet, but his expression showed his disgust. "Tell Patrick and Jane I'll be back this afternoon."

The elevator dinged, and Brightly and the two Electra members stepped in, with the ghost of Eden right behind them.

Twenty

When they reached the lobby, Delta was sitting cross-legged on the settee. Several mortals had joined her in the waiting area. Eden wondered if they, too, were here to report information on Brightly's daughter.

Delta's enormous eyes nearly popped out of their sockets when she saw Eden trailing Brightly and the women.

"I have to go with them!" Eden called across the lobby. It was strange being able to speak at any volume and know that only Delta could hear her.

Everyone could see and hear Delta, though. She seemed to want to intervene, but she restrained herself.

"Who's that woman staring at us?" Sylvana asked as they exited the building.

"Who knows?" Brightly dismissed.

"Heloise, do you recognize her?"

Eden frowned. Heloise was the name of a genie

alum, but in the course guide, her portrait was of a woman with wispy brown hair, a round face, and a bashful expression. She must have done a total overhaul for her thousandth wish.

Outside, Sylvana indicated a limousine waiting at the curb. "Our ride," she said, opening the back door.

Thinking fast, Eden jumped in ahead of the others, and slid all the way down the long leather seat. Brightly struggled to get in; the burn really seemed to be hurting him. Once he made it inside, he scooted all the way down, too. Eden had to slide off the seat and sit on the floor of the limo.

"Back to headquarters," Sylvana said to the driver. She reached up and slammed the divider shut, then settled back into her seat next to Brightly.

Eden's skin tingled with excitement. *They were going to Electra!*

Hopefully the Loyals wouldn't be annoyed that the plan had changed. But if they were, it wouldn't last once she came back with the kind of valuable information she expected to find.

It was too bad she didn't have a way to communicate with them. She didn't know how long she was going to be gone, and the Loyals would have to wait at Brightly Tech with no information about where she was. But Eden was sure that at some point Brightly would return to his office, and she could hitch a ride with him.

She turned her attention to the back of the limo. Sylvana was using a mirror to reapply her lipstick. She snapped her compact closed and smiled beguilingly at Brightly.

"David," she said, "I can't wait for you to see Electra."

The limo pulled up to a three-story building with columns and a white stone exterior.

"Here we are!" Sylvana announced.

They entered through a large glass door, opened for them by a suited doorman, into a high-ceilinged entryway with spotless white floors. In the middle stood a large marble sculpture of a woman in a one-shouldered robe, reaching one hand elegantly toward the sky. Eden couldn't help noticing how much she resembled an Electric alum named Kingsley.

Through the entryway was a desk where inquiring potential buyers spoke to receptionists. As they entered, the appearance of Sylvana and Heloise with Brightly caused a shift in the atmosphere. The receptionists sat up straighter and adjusted their chic eyeglasses. Guards stationed in discreet positions gave them respectful nods.

Behind reception was an open area with a grand staircase on each side. Standing in the middle, you could look up and see the second and third floors. Everything was white with gold accents: white marble floors, white walls, gold banisters, a textured gold ceiling. Gold-plated signs informed visitors that the first floor featured a viewing of Paris Jewels, and on the second was twentieth-century Asian art. Several galleries were connected to the room, and well-dressed Parisians milled about.

"Tonight, everything you see on this floor will be sold at the auction." Sylvana's heels clicked on the floor as she led Brightly into a gallery to the right. Heloise walked off in the opposite direction.

Eden was glad Sylvana couldn't see the way she was gaping. She'd thought Electra was only *called* an auction house so it could function as a front for Sylvana's lamp hunt. She hadn't realized the company actually purchased art or ran sales. *Au contraire,* she realized: Electra was a thriving operation.

Glass cases as high as Eden's chest displayed absurdly exquisite jewelry. Keeping up with Sylvana and Brightly, she peered into one with a long pearl necklace with a diamond clasp. Along with the sale date was an estimate of the price it would be sold for: three to four hundred thousand euros.

"Originally that was owned by Princess Marie Leszczynska," Sylvana told Brightly. "She married Louis XV."

"Exquisite," Brightly murmured. "How did y'all get your hands on it?"

"My friend Valentina sold it to us. When Princess Marie died, her son inherited it—and gave it to my friend's..." She cocked her head. "Well, one of her ancestors. It's been in Valentina's family for the past two hundred years."

It was a good thing no one could hear her, because Eden burst out laughing. Valentina was a genie alum who'd left the lamp in AD 543. She certainly didn't have any ancestors on Earth. The person the pearl necklace had been given to two hundred years ago must have been *her*.

Brightly admired it. "Why's she sellin' it?"

Sylvana shrugged. "It's good to keep the market moving. There are always more beautiful things." She smiled at a large man with a bushy beard as he walked past. *"Ça va, monsieur?"*

They moved on to the next display, a ruby ring with a diamond-covered band. The card identified it as being from the collection of Marie Antoinette. "This is one of my favorite pieces," Sylvana mused. "It reminds me of the old days in centuries past. Paris used to be so much more *elegant.*"

"I'd have to say I wouldn't know," Brightly said.

"Well, naturally. But, you know, that's what I *imagine*," Sylvana said, beaming a thousand-watt smile as she tossed her hair. "Don't you think?"

They looked at a sapphire-and-emerald brooch

before moving on to the next gallery. "It's going to be a good sale tonight," Sylvana said. "I hope you'll agree to attend, and sit by my side."

"By your side?" Brightly's voice went up an octave.

"Yes." Sylvana caressed his arm. "Would you be my date for the evening?"

A goofy grin spread across Brightly's face. "I'd be honored!"

Eden shook her head, repulsed.

Heloise was in the next gallery they entered. She was speaking in a hushed voice to a handsome dark-skinned man as he inspected an ornately designed diamond bracelet.

"Can you excuse me for one moment?" Sylvana left Brightly looking at a pair of yellow diamond earrings, and nodded to Heloise to step aside with her. Eden followed so she could hear their conversation.

"Is everything ready for tonight?" Sylvana asked Heloise.

"Yes."

"Where have we placed Mr. Yurislav and his guests?"

"In the last skybox."

"Wonderful. Make sure their champagne is well chilled. He is interested in the bracelet that belonged to Maria Theresa."

"He may have to contend with Mr. Modi." Heloise

nodded toward the man she'd been speaking to, who was still eying the same display.

"I'd love to break two hundred thousand euros on that."

"I'd say that's likely."

"Where is Madame Renegal going to be seated?"

"Third row middle."

"Good."

"And Monsieur Brightly?" Heloise asked. "Where will he sit?"

"Between you and me." Sylvana's eyes flashed.

"Très bien." Heloise's pouty lips curled up in what Eden supposed was a smile. "Seems like everything's moving along?"

"I think it's safe to say he's ours." Sylvana looked over at Brightly, who stood over a glass case across the gallery. She motioned that she'd be back in a moment, and he gave her a dopey grin. She turned back to Heloise and cringed. "I'm going to speed things along," she whispered. "I'll take him to lunch and see what I can learn."

"Sylvana," Heloise said admiringly, "you're very good at what you do."

"What can I say?" Sylvana smirked. *"Au revoir."* She and Heloise kissed each other on both cheeks.

Eden thought she might gag. All three of them were despicable. But it was clear that Sylvana was up to something—and Eden had a front-row seat to the action.

Sylvana approached Brightly and touched his arm. "Shall we move along? I've taken the liberty of making us a lunch reservation."

"Are you familiar with Avenue Montaigne?" Sylvana asked Brightly as they moved down the gray stone sidewalk. Brightly limped along slowly, leaning on his cane. Unbeknownst to them, Eden was following closely behind.

"To tell you the truth, I don't get out much," said Brightly. "Most of the time, I'm stuck in the office."

"But that's tragic! You're in Paris!" For once, Eden had to agree with Sylvana. Living in this city and spending your days in that office seemed like a waste. "Let me introduce you to my favorite street in the city."

It *was* a nice street. It was lined with rows of trees, with expensive-looking retail stores behind them. Eden recognized some of the brand names from her stroll up Fifth Avenue the first day she'd arrived in New York.

They reached a tan building with seven stories of windows. Beneath each window was a small round balcony adorned with a red geranium plant climbing over its black iron fence.

"Here we are," Sylvana said, approaching the door.

Above it were the words GRAND HOTEL PARIS in gold. Eden followed, taking the space behind Brightly's in the revolving door.

Inside, the white marble floor was patterned with inlaid designs in gold and soft blue. In the center was a dramatic display of white and red flowers on blocks of white marble that stood taller than Eden. To the left and right were long wooden concierge desks.

Eden looked at it all in awe. Though she didn't care much for this over-the-top luxurious style, she couldn't help being impressed.

"This is my favorite hotel in the city," Sylvana explained as she led the way through the lobby, nodding to the hotel employees. Through the entryway was a hallway with very large paintings that looked like they should be hanging in museums. As they crossed it, a familiar dark-haired woman rushed toward them excitedly.

"Sylvana!" Violet said as she approached.

"Violet," Sylvana said with disdain. "Can't you see I'm with a guest?"

Violet's happy expression faded. "Sorry," she said.

Eden rolled her eyes. It was pathetic how Violet seemed to live for Sylvana's approval.

"This is V," Sylvana said flatly. "She works for Electra too."

"Bonjour." Brightly looked disinterested.

"V's the kind of employee who's so dependable, you forget she's there," Sylvana said. There was a cruel glint in her eyes. "Like a reliable old dog."

Brightly laughed. "I've got a few like that too."

Sylvana sighed pityingly at Violet. "Now, leave us be!" She tossed her hair behind her shoulder and strutted off with Brightly.

Eden hung back for a moment. Violet looked like she was about to burst into tears—and for good reason. Why did she let Sylvana treat her that way?

Violet hurried off in the direction of the restroom. As Eden watched her go, she felt a pang of pity for her.

But she couldn't be distracted. She rushed to catch up with Sylvana and Brightly, who were now in the restaurant in the courtyard.

"All my employees from out of town stay at this hotel when they come to Paris," Sylvana said as the maître d' seated them at a table. "V and a few others are here for the auction." Luckily there were four chairs, so Eden slid into one right between them.

Sylvana and Brightly rattled off their orders to the waiter, who then left them alone.

"David, I'm so glad we met this morning." Sylvana batted her eyes. "It was so *rude* of me to show up at your office with no appointment—but when I found out you were in town, I just *had* to make sure you came to the showing."

"It's been my pleasure." Brightly sighed dramatically. "It's helped take my mind off everything that's going on."

Concern flooded Sylvana's bright turquoise eyes. It might have looked genuine to most people, but Eden knew this charade.

"Your daughter. I wanted to ask you about that. Are you okay?"

Scorn flashed across Brightly's face before he switched on a sad expression. He wasn't nearly as good an actor as Sylvana.

"I'm devastated," he said. "Eden means everything to me."

Eden had to laugh. Even though his delivery was unconvincing, the very fact that those words had come out of his mouth was ridiculous.

"I'm sure," Sylvana said. "I can't imagine how hard that must be." She was playing along like a pro.

The waiter brought over a few tiny plates of artfully styled appetizers. Greedily, Brightly snatched a few shells off a plate of escargot.

"If you don't mind me asking . . . how did it happen?" Sylvana nibbled delicately on a tart. "She was at home with you, and then when you woke up in the morning . . . she was gone?"

"Pretty much," Brightly answered, focusing his attention on the escargot.

"Don't you have security at your home here?"

"Well, yes," Brightly said. "Of course, it's not as good as what we have in California, where we usually live."

Sylvana folded her hands and leaned forward. "Can I tell you something, Mr. Brightly?"

Brightly met her eyes warily.

"I've been looking for Eden too," she said quietly. "For her, *and* for the lamp."

The blood drained from Brightly's face. The words sent a chill through Eden too.

The waiter appeared to serve their entrées: a steak, cooked rare, for Sylvana; and for Brightly, coq au vin: chicken cooked in wine, with mushrooms and onions.

Sylvana picked up her fork and knife and cut a razor-thin slice off her fillet. The meat inside was nearly bloodred. She placed it in her mouth and closed her eyes in delight as she chewed.

"What do you think of that, Mr. Brightly?" She smiled and patted her lips with her napkin.

"I—I'm afraid I don't know what you're talkin' about." Brightly looked like he'd lost his appetite.

Sylvana raised her eyebrows. "Really? You don't know that Eden is a genie?"

Brightly glanced around the restaurant nervously. But Sylvana went on.

"You're telling me you didn't meet her when you rubbed an antique oil lamp?"

"Shhh!" He eyed the other patrons to see if anyone had heard, but no one seemed to be paying attention.

"Fine," he whispered. "I rubbed the lamp."

"Aha! Now we're getting somewhere." Sylvana grinned and sliced off another piece of meat. "So, let me guess. You rubbed the lamp, and Eden the genie showed up and granted you three wishes. But you weren't happy with the way she granted them, and you didn't really get what you wanted. So now you're trying to find her so you can have another chance."

Brightly shook his head slowly. "Not exactly."

Sylvana swallowed. You could see she'd been caught by surprise—something that probably didn't happen often. "Well then, what?" she asked.

Brightly leaned back in his chair. Now that his secret was out, he was beginning to look more comfortable. He picked up his silverware and started to cut his chicken.

"Why should I tell you?" he asked.

Sylvana's eyes glowed. She licked her lips. "Because I could help you."

"Really?" he asked dubiously. "How?"

"I know everything about the lamp. All its secrets." She leaned forward. "If you can track down Eden, I can help you access the lamp's power. Forget about three wishes—you and I could share *unlimited* wishes."

Ice-cold fear shot through Eden. She knew Sylvana

was determined to obtain the lamp's power, but the only way that could happen was if Eden removed her genie bracelet. In San Diego, Eden had been able to hold her off. But if Sylvana teamed up with Brightly, who had the world's most advanced technology at his fingertips, things were sure to become more difficult.

"I'm intrigued," Brightly admitted, pushing his plate away.

"I'm sure you are," Sylvana purred. "You're an intelligent man, Mr. Brightly." She leaned forward. "Why don't you tell me what happened?"

He explained how he'd learned about the lamp from Reginald Clarke in Jamaica, then spent the past year trying to track it down. Once he got it, he said, he'd brought it to his lab here in Paris and rubbed it. And before he got around to making his wishes, Eden had escaped.

He told part of the truth, but he left out a lot of details. For instance, he didn't explain how he and his employees had performed medical tests on Eden. He also left out the part about the Veritas—as well as the fact that his scientist had placed a plasma shield around the lamp.

"How did she escape?" Sylvana asked.

"She used a laser to set fire to a bunch of oxygen tanks," Brightly said. "*And* she burned my leg. That's why I'm walkin' with this stupid cane." He scowled.

"Then, while my staff were helping me and putting out the fire, she cut a hole in the wall and jumped. From nine stories up!"

Nine stories up, Eden thought. So there *was* a level above where she'd been this morning. But how did you get there? The elevator only went to the eighth floor.

Brightly shook his head. "I don't know how she survived that."

"She's immortal," Sylvana said. "That's how." They both fell silent as the waiter arrived to collect their plates. Once he was gone, she asked: "So you didn't make *any* wishes?"

"No."

"And what about the lamp? I assume she took it with her?"

"No, I still have the lamp."

Sylvana froze in disbelief. "You *do*?"

"Yeah." He sighed. "Doesn't do me much good, though, without the genie. I tried makin' a wish after she left, but it didn't work."

"She has to be able to hear the wish," Sylvana murmured. "But it doesn't make sense that she was able to leave the lamp behind."

"Why not?"

"Never mind." Sylvana flashed him a winning smile. "Mr. Brightly, I want to help you. Together, we can make the lamp's power our own."

"How?"

"All we need are the genie and her lamp. So we're halfway there—more than halfway, really, because I'm sure she's still sneaking around Paris somewhere. In fact, I bet she's closer than we'd guess."

Eden swallowed. Sylvana had no idea how right she was.

"And you already have the lamp." Sylvana was radiant with excitement. "So what do you say?"

When Eden looked at Brightly to see his response, she saw that his eyes were downcast, as if he was looking at something just under the table. Curiously, she stood up to see what it was.

Beneath the table, Brightly's phone was in his hand. On the screen, a green line was zigzagging up and down.

He'd been watching it as Sylvana spoke—just like he and Jane had watched the electronic tablets while they interviewed Eden in Brightly Tech.

Eden couldn't believe it. He was using the Brightly Veritas!

"You're tellin' me that you know how to take the lamp's power?" he asked.

"Exactly."

His eyes dropped again. "How do you know all this?"

Sylvana smirked. "You wouldn't believe me if I told you."

"Well, maybe if we make this deal, you can try me."

"Absolutely," Sylvana said with spirit.

The green line on Brightly's phone plummeted from the top to the very bottom, then back again.

"Would we split that power evenly?"

"Of course! Fifty-fifty. We'll be partners."

Brightly looked up at Sylvana.

"All right," he said. "Tonight, after the auction, you can come to my lab and see the lamp."

"Oh!" Sylvana clapped her hands together ecstatically. "I can't wait to see it again!"

"And then, you can tell me everything you know." He pushed up his glasses and fixed his eyes on hers. "I'm dyin' to know the truth about all this."

"And *I* am dying to tell you." Sylvana's eyes twinkled with the joy of having ensnared yet another mortal. And all the while, under the table, the monitor on Brightly's phone continued its jagged dance.

When they went their separate ways, Eden hopped into the car that came for Brightly. It was clear that Sylvana intended to use him so she could attempt once again to get the lamp's power for herself. But there was no chance she was actually planning to partner with

Brightly. The idea of Sylvana splitting the lamp's power with a mortal was laughable.

Although it was easy to see Sylvana's motives, Eden wanted to learn more about Brightly's. From the way the green line had shot all over the screen, she was guessing that the Veritas had detected Sylvana's lies. And yet, Brightly had agreed to partner with her.

Maybe Sylvana wasn't the only one being deceitful.

In the car, Brightly slid the partition closed and dialed a number on his cell phone. After two rings, Jane Johnston's face appeared on the screen.

"Where are you?" she demanded. "I've been trying to reach you for hours!"

Eden leaned over to get a closer look. It was just like a message from the masters, but in real time!

"I'll explain," Brightly said. "Any update on the girl?"

"No. A couple crazies with dead-end leads." Jane rolled her eyes. "Where have you been? Marguerite said you left the office with two women."

"The president and CEO of Electra paid me a visit."

"Electra?" Jane said. "What's that?"

"An auction house. They're holdin' a sale tonight, and I went to the showing with them."

"*Why?*"

"They know about Eden."

Jane looked astonished. "They know *what*?"

"That she's a genie. At least, one of them does."

"How?"

"I don't know. She said she wants to partner with me. She claims she can tap into the lamp's power and get us both unlimited wishes."

Jane gasped. "Is that true?"

"No," Brightly answered bitterly. "I activated the Veritas, and the meter was goin' bananas. Her dishonesty was off the charts."

Finally, Sylvana had been caught in a lie! Eden was delighted.

"She's tryin' to use me to get what she wants," Brightly said. "Jane, why are people always tryin' to use me?"

"David," Jane said, "you're brilliant and wealthy. It's inevitable that people will try to take advantage of you."

"But why do they have to *lie* to me?" Brightly shrieked. Eden grimaced. She was pretty sure there was another tantrum coming.

"David," Jane said, "I want you to take three breaths and focus."

Eden watched as Brightly inhaled deeply, then exhaled three times in a row.

"Better?" Jane asked.

Brightly nodded.

"Now. Do you think there's a chance that this woman—what was her name?"

"Sylvana."

"Do you think you could get more information from her? If she knew about the genie, she *must* know more about the lamp and its power. Don't you think?"

"That's why I'm gonna bring her to the lab tonight. I told her she can come see the lamp, and we'll talk business."

That piqued Jane's interest. "Are we going to—"

"Yep. Just like we did for Eden."

Jane rubbed her hands together eagerly. "What time is she coming?"

"About nine, I'd guess. After the auction at Electra. Which I'll be attendin'."

"David, are you sure? Wouldn't it look bad for you to be there? Remember, you're supposed to be searching for your missing daughter."

"I don't think my being there will weaken the story. An appearance will keep it in the public eye. That way, people will keep lookin'—and it'll be more likely that someone will spot her." Brightly sniffed. "Once I get that genie back, there's gonna be a Veritas in every phone on the planet. No one will ever get away with lyin' to me again."

"If things go well tonight," Jane said, "you might not need to make that wish. You might learn how to make as many wishes as you want."

Brightly smiled that toothy grin. "You've got a good

point there." The car pulled to a stop, and he looked out the window. "I'm at the office," he said.

"Good. Come up and meet me in the lab," said Jane.

"Okay. See you in a sec."

He climbed out of the car, and Eden slipped out behind him. Her heart was racing. Already she had so much to tell the Loyals—and now, she was going to learn how to get to the lab!

But right as she stepped up to the revolving door, wiry arms encircled her waist.

"Hey!" She looked up and saw Delta's face, set in determination. Her hair was waving wildly in the breeze. "What are you doing?" Eden demanded.

Delta didn't answer—just dragged her to the brown Renault parked around the corner. She opened the back door and shoved Eden inside.

Twenty-One

"What were you thinking?" Bola roared. The old car's transmission struggled with the steep inclines on the way into Montmartre; it strained and rumbled as they went. Bola raised her voice over it. "We've been sitting there waiting for hours! Why on Earth would you leave Brightly Tech?"

"I had to!" Eden said. "Sylvana and Heloise were there with Brightly. I went to Electra with them!"

It wouldn't be safe for her to be visible until they were back in the house, so Delta was still the only one who could see or hear her. In the backseat beside her, she raised her eyebrows. "I hope you got something we can use."

"I did!" Eden insisted.

"What is she saying?" Bola yelled.

"She said she did," Delta said.

"Well, what? Does she know how to get to the lab?"

Eden bit her lip. Although she'd learned that the lab was on the ninth floor, she still didn't know how to access it. "Well, not exactly, but—"

"No," Delta said to Bola.

"But I was about to! Right before you dragged me away!"

Bola started in on a fiery new rant. Meanwhile, in the front passenger seat, Pepper stayed silent. Eden watched her guardian's face in the rearview mirror. Usually Pepper's face broadcasted every thought that crossed her mind. But for the first time, Eden couldn't read her at all.

Back at the house, once Delta had made Eden visible, the Loyals sat around the table while she recounted everything she'd seen and heard. Trevor sat curled in Delta's lap, and the zebra finches perched on her shoulders alongside a green parakeet and a cockatiel.

"Are you absolutely sure he's going to attend the auction tonight?" Bola asked.

"Yes," Eden said. "And then he's going to bring Sylvana back to Brightly Tech and question her with the Veritas."

Bola breathed in deeply through her nostrils. "Then it's essential that we retrieve the lamp while they're at Electra."

"Exactly." Eden nodded enthusiastically. "I can be invisible again."

Bola blinked. "Well obviously *you're* not going to go."

"What do you mean?"

Bola's laugh was short and harsh. "Do you really think we'd let you come after what happened today? Eden, you didn't follow instructions."

Eden's mouth dropped open in disbelief. "That was the only way I could have learned what I did!" she protested. "If I hadn't gone, we wouldn't know that Sylvana's trying to use Brightly to get the lamp. And we wouldn't know that he'll be at the auction tonight!"

"It was *incredibly* irresponsible for you to leave Brightly Tech." Bola's English accent made her words sharp as daggers. "Your sole objective was to learn how to access the lab, and you failed."

"If you hadn't followed them," Delta said, "you would have had a perfect opportunity to explore the facility without Brightly there."

"Exactly," Bola spat. "Did you think about that?"

"Now when we go in tonight, we're going to have to figure it out as we go," Delta said irritably.

"I'm *sorry*," Eden said. "I thought I was doing the right thing."

"Well you weren't," Bola snapped. "You were being selfish, as usual. Chasing after whatever you pleased instead of thinking of the people who are trying to help you. And as a result, you've heightened the risk for us all."

Eden smacked her palm on the table. "That's so unfair!"

"Unfair?" Bola hissed. "Eden, you proved what I suspected: that you can't handle this type of thing."

Eden blinked back indignant tears. She turned to Pepper, who was sitting silently beside her.

"Pepper, tell her I can do it!"

Pepper was staring at the table. She looked up and gazed sadly at Eden. "You know I love you, kid. But Bola's right. You should sit this one out."

Eden felt a sob rise up in her chest. She shoved her chair back, ran up the red-carpeted stairs and into the bedroom, and threw herself on the saggy bed.

She must have cried herself to sleep, because she woke up a while later with puffy eyes and a dry mouth. Looking at her phone, she saw that several hours had passed.

Eden rolled onto her back and stared at the ceiling. She'd been *lucky* to happen upon Brightly with the Electric. How could Bola and the others possibly blame her for following them after hearing what she'd found out? She would have been crazy to let them slip away!

She pouted and crossed her arms. She felt wronged by everyone, but most of all Pepper. She knew the Loyals were narrow-minded and stuck in their ways, so in a way, their reaction was no surprise. But now Pepper was acting just like them!

In New York, Pepper and Eden had roamed the city without a care in the world. But now Pepper was being just as stuffy, mean, and boring as the rest of them.

"Eden?" Pepper's voice came from the other side of the bedroom door.

"What?" Eden asked flatly.

Pepper was silent for a moment. Then: "We've got things for sandwiches downstairs. Do you want to come make one?"

"I'm not hungry." It was a lie, of course; she hadn't eaten since breakfast, and it was now late afternoon. But she didn't feel like seeing any of them.

"Do you want me to bring one up here for you?"

"I said I'm not *hungry*."

Pepper cleared her throat. "All right. Can I come in?"

Eden didn't answer. Pepper opened the door and poked her head inside. She'd tied a colorful scarf around her mop of curls.

"What's on your head?"

"Do you like it? I found it in a little store on the way to the market." A smile started to spread across Pepper's face.

But Eden wasn't ready to make friends again.

"It's different," she said coldly.

Pepper crept forward and sat on the edge of the bed. "You know, I didn't mean to hurt your feelings." Eden's eyes flicked up to meet hers, then back down again. In that moment, she could see that Pepper truly meant it. Still, that didn't make what had happened okay.

Eden narrowed her eyes at her. "If you didn't want to hurt my feelings, you should have stood up for me earlier."

"But to some extent, what Bola said was *true*," Pepper said. The gentle tone of her voice made Eden even angrier. "You have to realize that. You didn't follow the plan we'd agreed upon."

Eden rolled her eyes. "But I was *fine*." She couldn't understand what the big deal was.

Pepper sighed and pulled off the colorful head scarf. She kept her eyes on her hands as she folded and unfolded it. "You know, Xavier and Goldie asked me to look after you. That means that you need to listen to me, even if what I say isn't what you want to do. I'm your guardian. It's my job to keep you safe."

Eden eyed her bitterly. "And here I thought you were my friend."

Pepper winced, but Eden didn't care. Pepper's words had hurt her, too.

"Pepper," Bola said, stopping in the doorway, "let's eat so we can get going. We need to be out of there long before he's back from the auction."

Pepper turned and nodded to her. Bola's eyes skimmed over Eden, but she didn't say anything more— just turned and went down the stairs.

"I love you, kid," Pepper said.

Eden crossed her arms and faced the window. She couldn't believe they were leaving her behind.

After about thirty seconds, she heard Pepper sigh. Then the saggy bed squeaked as her guardian stood up and left.

Twenty-Two

When Violet arrived at Electra headquarters, the air was buzzing with anticipation. The auction was set to start in half an hour.

Mortal employees wearing black from head to toe drifted through the halls, speaking quietly and eying everyone. Arriving attendees flitted around greeting one another with air kisses, trying to impress one another with little bits of news about their fabulous lives.

Naturally, all attendees were dressed to the nines, including Violet. She was wearing a strapless navy gown, and her dark hair was pulled into a chignon. The final touches were a necklace with a ruby the size of a grape hanging from it, and a ruby ring to match.

But she was miserable. What Sylvana had said in the hotel lobby had ruined her day. Hearing Heloise named CEO last night had been bad, but what had happened today was far worse. Sylvana had insulted Violet right in front of her! Called her an old dog!

The salesroom where the auction would be held was on Electra's second story. The room was grand and spacious, with high walnut banquettes running along its perimeter. When Violet entered, a mortal Electra employee showed her to a seat in the front row.

Most people in the room would have been honored to sit here, but for Violet, it was yet another insult. She gazed up to the banquette, where she *should* be. The three empty seats closest to the stage were reserved for the most important people in the room. Tonight, there was no question who that was.

As the auction's final attendees arrived, Sylvana and Heloise made their entrance. Each of them held one of David Brightly's elbows, although for some reason he was walking with a cane. Violet had noticed that earlier at the hotel, too.

As they stopped along the way for obligatory air kisses, the women looked like movie stars at a film premiere. Sandwiched between them, Brightly beamed shamelessly.

Whispers rippled through the salesroom. Everyone would know about the disappearance of Brightly's daughter—and yet, here he was, looking like the happiest man in Paris.

Violet watched Electra's new CEO take the seat nearest to the stage.

That should be me, she thought bitterly.

A stately middle-aged gentleman in a suit took the stage, standing behind a tall wooden podium. Gold letters on the front spelled ELECTRA. The room fell quiet as he began.

"This is sale 2857, Paris Jewels," he said in French. "Lots 1 through 117. We'll begin the bidding with Lot 1." Above the stage, the wall rotated to showcase a pair of yellow diamond earrings. A screen above the auctioneer showed a close-up view of the piece. "Diamond Cartier earrings from 1932, shown on the screen behind me, and also pictured and described in your catalogues. We'll start the bidding at forty thousand euros. Forty thousand?" A short-haired woman raised a red card to place a bid. "Forty-one thousand." And the show was under way.

Violet hadn't been to an auction in years, but she'd always enjoyed their fast pace and elite nature. But this time, she couldn't concentrate on anything except the banquette.

Heloise was as pouty and listless as usual. Brightly smiled widely, showing his big white teeth. And Sylvana sat coolly, regal as a queen.

"Lot 19. The diamond bracelet once owned by

Maria Theresa of Spain, the first wife of Louis XIV." The image of the intricately designed bracelet appeared on the screen. Several bidders sat up straighter. There had been a lot of buzz about this item; it was one of the most highly valued items in the auction.

"We'll start the bidding at one hundred thousand euros. One hundred thousand?"

A man raised his paddle but was quickly outbid by a woman on a phone. Some of the "regulars" who were known to make large purchases were placed in private skyboxes that looked down on the salesroom from a floor above. While enjoying food and drinks served by Electra catering staff, they communicated by phone to agents on the floor who placed bids for them.

As bidders battled over the bracelet, Violet noticed something unusual in the banquette. Mr. Brightly was whispering agitatedly to Sylvana, who seemed perturbed by whatever he was saying. Her perfectly plucked eyebrows furrowed with concern.

"Sold!" the auctioneer declared. "The diamond bracelet once belonging to Maria Theresa, for two hundred forty thousand euros. To Mr. Yurislav, up in the skybox." He pointed above, and everyone clapped politely.

Brightly and Sylvana had risen to their feet and were squeezing past Heloise. They left the banquette and slipped out of the salesroom through the exit on that side.

Violet's pulse was racing. She'd never known Sylvana to leave an auction. Something important must have happened.

"And now, on to Lot 20: a turquoise, gold, and diamond brooch."

As the auction proceeded, the jewels for sale continued to enchant the other attendees.

But Violet would have given any precious gem in the world to know where Sylvana had gone.

Twenty-Three

As creepy as the Montmartre house had been before, it was even worse without other people in it.

Soon after the others left, Eden went downstairs to rummage around in Delta's kitchen. Like the rest of the house, it had seen better days. The floor was pale-green linoleum, and the counters were a gross orangey brown. But there was half a baguette on the counter, and in the refrigerator some sliced ham, mayonnaise, and a tomato. There was also a carton of milk, a jar of pickles, and a few cans of cat food.

"*Cat* food?" Eden wondered aloud. Was there a cat somewhere around here too?

She pulled out what she needed, made a sandwich, and poured herself a glass of milk. She took them to the dining table and sat there alone while she ate. None of Delta's pets were in sight—and, for once, they were silent, too.

When she was finished, Eden washed her dishes and placed them back in Delta's cabinets. Then she rooted around in the kitchen drawers. Among a wide variety of moldy-smelling junk, she found a pack of playing cards. She went into the other room downstairs, a living room with a strange assortment of furniture including a faded blue sofa and a harpsichord, and played solitaire while the sun set. Although the curtains were closed, the room got darker and darker as she played.

She won four games in a row, but then she couldn't see the suits anymore. She didn't feel like turning on the light, so she sat in the dark, sort of creeped out but also still angry, and wondered what was happening at Brightly Tech.

An hour later, most of the animals had joined Eden downstairs. Clearly, they weren't used to Delta being away. Trevor the dog whined; the birds cheeped and squawked; and the cat, who'd made her first appearance, mewed plaintively. Eden went back into the kitchen to find food for all of them, then set out their meals in bowls and dishes and watched the animals inhale them.

By now, she would have expected Pepper, Bola, and Delta to be back. She wasn't worried, exactly; they were immortal, so nothing could really happen to them. Still, it seemed strange that they weren't home yet.

She went upstairs and into the bedroom she was

sharing with Pepper. Right as she sat on the saggy bed, she heard a car pull up in front of the house and stop.

She wanted to rush to the window, but instead, she made herself stay seated. She didn't want them to see she'd been worried. She wanted to give off the appearance of being cool and unconcerned.

A car door slammed. Downstairs, the animals were going crazy—squawking, barking, and meowing. Had they done that earlier today when they came home? Eden couldn't remember.

She couldn't hold out any longer. She went to the window and peeked through the curtain. And what she saw sucked the breath out of her chest.

The car parked in front of the derelict house wasn't Delta's banged-up brown Renault. Instead, it was a sleek black sedan exactly like the one Eden had hopped into with Brightly.

Downstairs, the gold door knocker banged. The animals went even more mental. Eden crept halfway down the stairs.

"Are you sure this is right?" a man asked in French. "It sounds like a zoo in there."

"This is the address that old Renault was registered to," a woman responded.

Eden clapped a hand over her mouth. The old Renault was Delta's car!

"The registration is thirty years old," the woman

went on, "but it doesn't look like this place has changed since then."

The man could be Dr. Patrick Evans or Jean Luc. At any rate, Eden was sure she hadn't heard Brightly's drawling voice. And the woman could only be Jane Johnston.

"I don't understand why she'd be with those women—and at this house," said the man.

"But you saw the photo that the little one had on her," said Jane. "That was definitely a picture of Eden. Trust me, we're at the right place."

Eden's heart pounded. Pepper must have brought the photo of Eden and Tyler with her! But she never would have offered it up to Brightly's employees willingly. If they'd seen it, that meant...

"Anyone home?" Jane's voice called. She banged the door knocker again, and the animals went ballistic. "Hello!"

Eden scrambled up the rest of the stairs and into the bedroom, and locked the door. She surveyed the room wildly, thinking fast.

She flung the closet door open and saw the brown wig on a shelf. She used an elastic on her wrist to twist her hair into a low bun, then pulled it on.

The school uniform was hanging in the closet too, but the growing intensity of the knocking downstairs told her she didn't have time to worry about that.

Pepper had brought the leather backpack from New York, and most of the cash that the masters had placed inside was still there. That was American money, though. Eden saw Pepper's purse, pulled it over, and dug around to find her wallet. Peeking inside, she saw credit cards. She slipped one into the pocket of her jean shorts.

Pepper's new patterned head scarf was lying on the floor next to the purse. Eden swallowed when she saw it.

From downstairs, she heard a sharp crack, then a sound like glass shattering. The animals cranked up the volume of their chaotic cries, and Eden's heart started drumming harder and faster.

"Through here!" she heard Jane hiss. Then, louder: "Eden?"

In the bedroom, Eden struggled to unlock the window. The latch on the pane was rusted closed; it probably hadn't been opened for decades. Still, she worked at it with trembling fingers.

"Eden! Where are you?" said the man in accented English. *Must be Jean Luc,* Eden thought. It didn't sound like Dr. Evans.

"What's with all these animals?" said Jane, sounding cranky.

"Eden! Your friends are at the lab. They want you to come!" Jean Luc called.

Even as she worked at the lock, Eden had to roll her eyes. Did they think she was stupid?

"Remember how you wanted Mr. Brightly to make his wishes? He's ready now." The stairs started to creak, and Jane's voice grew closer. "We'll take you to him, and then you can go home with your friends."

Just then, the latch flew open. It pinched Eden's finger, but the pain subsided immediately. She shoved the window up, sat on the ledge, and swung her feet out.

The doorknob clicked as someone tried to open it. "I think she's in here!" Jane exclaimed.

There was the sound of a blunt impact on the wood. Even with that first kick, Eden heard wood splinter. It wouldn't withstand much more.

Eden took a deep breath and launched herself out of the second-story window.

She landed softly enough on the small patch of grass in front of the house, but her right foot twisted when it hit the ground. It took all she had to suppress a scream of agony. Biting her lip, she lifted the foot and shook it out, and it returned to normal right away. She remembered how much pain Sasha had been in when she'd sprained her ankle at the beach in San Diego, and was overwhelmingly grateful for her genie bracelet's magical healing power.

She stole across the yard, moving downhill. She passed the handsome cream house with green shutters pressed up against Delta's. Then the next house, then another. She picked up speed as she flew down the steeply inclined road, with the cool September air grazing her skin.

She needed to get out of Montmartre. Once Jane and Jean Luc broke into the bedroom—and it wouldn't take long—they'd see that the window was open. She'd jumped from a much higher height at Brightly Tech, so they'd probably know that she'd done it again. And also, that she wasn't far away.

I need a taxi, she thought—but it seemed like a long shot among Montmartre's winding streets. Still, as she jogged through the night, she scanned them for a car with a lit-up sign on top. She had no idea where to go—but at the moment, anywhere was better than here.

The moon was nearly full, and a few stars illuminated the sky. She could see more of them here than in New York, anyway.

Jean Luc had said that "all her friends" were at Brightly Tech. Presumably, that meant Pepper, Bola, and Delta. Or was Sylvana being held there too? If things had gone according to Brightly's plan, she'd be trapped in his clutches right along with the Loyals.

Eden couldn't imagine how they'd managed to capture them all. It seemed that even without his wishes, Brightly was more powerful than Eden had realized.

Her friends. Who *were* Eden's friends, anyway? Bola and Delta? They'd been so angry when she'd followed Brightly and Sylvana to Electra. And what about

Pepper? The thought made Eden's heart ache. She'd felt so betrayed by Pepper. But deep down, she knew her guardian was trying to protect her. And the truth was, it had worked. If Eden had gone with them, she'd probably be trapped in Brightly Tech too.

Eden remembered how she'd acted when Pepper left, and was hit by a sick sense of shame. She'd been horrible. Pepper had told her she loved her, and she hadn't even answered.

Somehow, she had to get them out. And as she veered down the tiniest streets she could find, it was clear that she was going to need help. But from who?

She thought about the people who'd helped her so far. There was Melodie, the master of disguise. Though Eden had been to her house, there was no chance she could navigate her way back there. And anyway, she couldn't risk attracting the attention of her journalist parents.

Tyler and Sasha were halfway across the world—and since she hadn't checked her online profile since she'd messaged them, she didn't know if they'd responded. There was a very good chance they wanted nothing to do with her.

There was absolutely no one to turn to. Eden was at a loss.

But then, something occurred to her. *She* might not have any other friends in Paris, but Sylvana did. And if the night had gone according to Brightly's plans, Sylvana needed help just as badly as the Loyals.

The idea starting to form in Eden's head was an odd one. And yet, she realized grimly, it might be her only chance.

Just then, a taxi appeared. Eden waved her arms frantically to flag it down.

She climbed in and spoke to the driver in French: "Take me to the Grand Hotel Paris."

Twenty-Four

Outside the hotel on Avenue Montaigne, Eden paid using Pepper's credit card and took a moment to adjust her wig before getting out of the car. She looked up at the red geraniums climbing over the hotel's balconies, and summoned all the courage she could muster.

She entered through the revolving door. In a perfect world, she'd march through the lobby and proceed straight on to her destination. But unfortunately, she didn't know where that destination was. So instead, she sidled up to the long wooden desk.

"*Bonsoir, mademoiselle,*" said a sour-faced young woman with very thin eyebrows.

"*Bonsoir,*" Eden replied. She continued in French. "My aunt asked me to bring something to her assistant, but she forgot to tell me which room she's in."

"*Pas de problème,*" the woman said. "Give me her name, and I'll call up to her room."

"Actually, my aunt told me not to do that," Eden said. "She said I should go straight up."

The woman blinked at her. "That's impossible."

"Why?"

"I can't just give you a guest's room number."

"Oh, really?" Eden shook her head. "That's too bad. Aunt Sylvana won't be happy about that."

The woman raised her thin eyebrows. "Aunt *who*?"

"Sylvana. You know, the head of Electra?"

"She's your aunt?" The woman looked unconvinced.

"Yeah. She told me not to bother her tonight after the auction, but if you insist—"

"Yes, I would need to speak to her," the woman said icily. "We know Sylvana very well. Have her call us at the front desk."

Eden smiled, trying to appear unruffled.

"Pas de problème," she said. "Just a minute."

She walked through the lobby, took a left at the hallway filled with paintings, and sat on a plush navy armchair. She'd been hoping the name of her nemesis would work like a magic password. But she was learning that things were never quite as easy as she hoped.

She was glad to be out of the receptionist's line of sight. She didn't even have a phone to pretend she was trying to get ahold of Sylvana. She sighed, thinking of what to do next.

Her chair faced the door and several large windows to the courtyard where Sylvana and Brightly had eaten lunch. It was bustling with late-night revelers.

On the right side of the door sat one other person in an armchair. It looked like a boy, hunched over with his elbows on his legs, holding his head in his hands.

Eden couldn't see his face, but his hair was straight, shiny chestnut brown. At his feet was a gray-and-white backpack, emblazoned with the logo of a popular surf company.

Eden frowned. She'd seen that backpack before—or at least one exactly like it.

She stood up and crept over slowly. There was no chance in the world that it was him, she told herself. But for peace of mind, she had to make sure.

She stood over him, staring at the back of his head. It certainly looked like him from this angle. But there was no chance he'd be here in Paris.

If she were to say his name, she'd be embarrassed when it wasn't him. But she also couldn't seem to move away.

A laughing couple opened the door from the courtyard and walked inside, letting the merriment from outside leak in momentarily. The boy straightened up and shook his shaggy hair to one side.

When their eyes met, Eden felt as if a vacuum had sucked all the breath from her lungs.

"Tyler?" she gasped.

But in his face, she saw only confusion.

Eden was mortified. What if he'd come to Paris for some reason completely separate from her? What if he really didn't want to see her ever again? Or—even worse—what if he'd already forgotten her completely?

But then she remembered she was wearing the wig.

He jumped to his feet. "Eden!" he said. "I didn't even recognize you with that—"

"Shhhh," she said, clapping a hand over his mouth. The happy couple turned and glanced at them, but they didn't care enough to stop and investigate. They continued through the lobby.

Eden took her hand off Tyler's mouth. "You can't say my name," she whispered. "I'm in disguise at the moment. Because—"

"Because everyone's looking for you!" he said, more quietly. "I know, I'm sorry. That was stupid." He squeezed her shoulders, then took his hands away, looking nervous. "I—"

She reached out and hugged him as tight as she could. It was *him*! He was here, right now, in Paris!

"How are you *here*?" she whispered.

"I snuck away," he said earnestly. "Dad doesn't know—well, actually, he does now, and he's pissed. But I had to come. Sasha and I pooled all our money, and we had just enough for one ticket to Paris. But she doesn't have a passport, and I got one last year because I was going to go on a trip to Mexico with Devin and his family—before Mom got sick."

"But—*why?*" She still didn't dare presume...

"For *you!*" Tyler grinned, showing those slightly crooked teeth that Eden had missed so much. "To help you, I mean. Why else would I come to Paris?"

"*Really?*" Eden felt a kind of happiness she hadn't known existed. For some reason, it made her feel like she might cry. "Does this mean you're not mad at me?"

"Mad at you? Why?"

"Because of what happened last time, with your dad. It was all because of me."

Tyler laughed. "Are you crazy? That wasn't your fault! Sash and I *never* blamed you for that! Anyway, it all worked out okay."

Eden was weak with relief. It felt like she'd been carrying a backpack stuffed with heavy books for weeks, and she'd only just removed it.

"When we woke up yesterday morning, Sasha got your message," Tyler said. "We both wrote you, but you didn't answer. Then we saw that David Brightly was searching for you. We didn't know what was going on, but we knew it couldn't be good."

"You saw that all the way in San Diego?"

"Yeah! It's big news. Everyone was asking us about it at school."

Eden grimaced. She hadn't managed to fit in with the kids at Mission Beach Middle even when she was sitting next to them in classes, trying her best to blend in as a normal seventh grader. She couldn't imagine what they must be thinking now.

"And then I got a message from your friend Melodie."

Eden's mouth dropped open in surprise. "You *did?*"

"Yeah. It was in French, but I translated it on the Internet. She wanted to tell you she was sorry about what happened. Something about her sister showing up? Anyway, she thought you might be with me. And then I knew for sure that I had to come."

Eden's face felt warm. Maybe she had a few more friends than she'd thought.

"But how did you end up *here*, at this hotel?" That part Eden really couldn't make sense of.

"I remembered how you'd said that Electra's headquarters are in Paris, and that Sylvana had tried to bring you here. I knew that if something funny was going on, they were probably involved. I found out they were having an auction tonight, so I went. Well, they wouldn't let me inside, but I hung around outside looking for you." He tossed his head again to get the hair out of his eyes. "No sign of you, but I did see Violet. I was sure she'd recognize me, but she seemed like she was in her own world. She left by herself, so I followed her—and ended up here."

"Excusez-moi." The receptionist had come out from behind her desk and was standing in front of them. Her arms were crossed, and she looked suspicious. "Did you talk to your aunt?"

"Even better," Eden said. "I ran into my friend, and he knows where the assistant is staying. But thanks anyway, you've been great." The receptionist scowled, turned on her heel, and went back to her desk.

"You may not believe this," Eden whispered when she was gone, "but I came here tonight looking for Violet. Is there any chance at all that you followed her up to her room?"

"Yeah," Tyler said. "I couldn't believe she didn't notice me standing right next to her in the elevator, but she was totally oblivious. I watched her go into her room. She's in 707."

Eden hugged him again. "You're a miracle," she said. She tugged his hand, and started down the hall. "Let's go!"

Tyler picked up his backpack and followed. "We're going to her room?"

"Yeah!"

"But why?"

"Because she's going to help us. I hope." Eden pressed the button to call the elevator.

Twenty-Five

As the elevator rose, Eden explained the plan she had in mind.

"You think that will work?" Tyler asked.

Eden shrugged. "It's the best thing I can think of."

On the seventh floor, they followed the hall to room 707.

"Here goes nothing," Eden said. She took a deep breath and knocked.

"Who is it?" Violet's voice called.

Eden cleared her throat. "I need to talk to you. It's about Sylvana."

The door opened a crack, and Violet peeked through.

She certainly didn't look like she'd just been at a glamorous event. She wore a thick white hotel bathrobe, and her hair was in a messy topknot. She looked as unglamorous as Eden had ever seen her.

"Sylvana's in trouble," Eden said. "If you let me inside, I'll tell you more."

Violet squinted skeptically. "Do I know you?"

It was now or never, Eden supposed. She reached up and pulled the brown wig off her head.

"Yeah, you know me."

Violet gasped and flung the door open. "Get in here," she hissed.

Room 707 was actually a suite. Eden and Tyler entered into a living room dominated by a big crimson sofa, with two matching armchairs flanking it. They faced a formal coffee table with a dozen bloodred roses blooming in a vase on top.

The cream walls were paneled with gold trim and decorated with landscape paintings. A chandelier hung from above, and forest-green curtains blocked the view through the windows.

Violet stood in front of Eden and took in the sight of her. "It's really you," she marveled. "And you!" she exclaimed, moving to Tyler. Her face creased in thought. "Did I see you somewhere earlier tonight?"

"I came up in the elevator with you," he said.

"That's right! I thought you looked familiar. Now I remember: you're the boy from San Diego!"

Violet was the first alum Eden had ever met in

person, but they'd been adversaries from the start. After their first encounter on Mission Beach, conflicts had complicated Eden's time on Earth. She'd never dreamed she'd come to Violet for help. And obviously, neither had Violet.

"Why are you here?" she asked.

"It's a long story," Eden said. "But let's start with the most pressing thing first."

"Sylvana," Violet breathed. "Why did you say she's in trouble?"

"Can we sit?" Eden asked, indicating the sofa. Violet shrugged and took an armchair.

"I've been in Paris for almost forty-eight hours," Eden said as she and Tyler sat. "I was summoned here when David Brightly rubbed the lamp two nights ago. But the granting took a bad turn, and I couldn't make a request for reentry, so I escaped from his lab."

"Why couldn't you—"

"Like I said, it's a long story." Eden wanted to disclose as little as possible, while still convincing Violet to help. Most importantly, she wasn't going to tell her that she no longer lived in the lamp. "Brightly has covered the lamp with a plasma shield—basically, a force field. No one and nothing can go in or out, and I don't think the masters' telescope works either."

Violet's face lit up with interest. "Wow. I never would have thought a mortal—"

"Could outsmart the masters? I know, me neither. And I haven't even granted a wish for him yet."

"So what does this have to do with Sylvana?"

Eden swallowed. She'd have to tread carefully now. She knew that Violet had seen Sylvana with Brightly, but Violet obviously wasn't willing to offer up that information. Eden would be wise to keep her cards close too.

"I linked up with a few alumni in Paris. We've been working together to figure out how to get the lamp back. This morning we went back to Brightly Tech to do recon. I was invisible, thanks to a power granted by one of the alumni's thousandth wish. While I was there, I saw Sylvana and Heloise at the office with Brightly, and I followed them to Electra."

"You were at *Electra* this morning?"

"Yeah. I walked around with Sylvana and Brightly, then I went to lunch with them here at the hotel. Sylvana told him she has information about the lamp and proposed splitting its powers with him, fifty-fifty." Eden eyed Violet. "Although, as you and I both know, Sylvana would never actually split those powers with anyone—especially a mortal."

Violet stayed stone-faced. "Finish your story."

Eden leaned forward on the sofa. "The point is, Brightly knew that too! I rode in his car back to the office, and I heard him talking on the phone. He was planning to bring Sylvana to the lab tonight after the auction to show her the lamp, then trap her there and question her. And I think that's exactly what's happened."

Violet twisted a ruby ring on her index finger and thought for a minute. Finally, she shook her head. "I don't believe you," she said.

"*Why?*"

"*No one* can resist Sylvana. Why would this guy be different?"

"He wouldn't have been able to tell that she was lying on his own," Eden said. "But he was using this new technology he's developed." Eden explained about the Brightly Veritas—how he'd used it on her when he'd summoned her, and then on Sylvana at the restaurant.

Violet drummed her slender fingers on the side table. "How do I know you're not making this up? Even if you *were* invisible, you'd have to have some nerve to chase around two people who'd do anything to find you."

"I can prove it," Eden said.

"How?"

"I saw you."

Violet's eyebrows lifted. "Me?"

"Yeah. We passed you when we were going into the restaurant downstairs. Sylvana said some pretty rude things to Brightly about you. How you're so dependable, she forgets that you're there. And that you're like a reliable old dog."

With that, Violet looked like she'd seen a ghost. She stood up and started pacing around the room. "But—" Now that she'd gotten her proof, she was struggling to comprehend it all.

"Violet," Eden said, "tonight my friends went back to Brightly Tech to try to get the lamp, but I think they were caught. It might have even happened during the auction. Did anything unusual happen when you were there?"

Violet went a shade whiter. "Yes. Sylvana left early with Brightly."

"My guess is, he found out they'd infiltrated his lab. He must have brought Sylvana with him—but once he got her there, I bet she found herself in the same position as them. Have you heard from her since then?"

Violet shook her head.

"Well, don't take my word for it. Why don't you call her? See if she answers." If she was wrong and Brightly hadn't followed through with his plot to trap Sylvana, Eden was going to be in a very bad position. But she didn't think she was wrong.

Violet went into the suite's bedroom. Tyler took Eden's hand in his and squeezed it.

"So far, so good," he whispered.

She grinned. She still couldn't believe he was here.

Eden leaned over to peer into the bedroom. Inside was a huge bed, topped by a lace canopy. In one corner, a Louis Vuitton suitcase was open on a luggage rack.

Violet sat on the bed and pressed a few buttons on her phone, then held it to her ear. After fifteen seconds or so, she hung up. She tried again, with the same result.

"No answer?" Eden asked.

Violet came out to rejoin them. "No." She sat on the armchair again. "Let's say you *are* right," she said. "You still haven't answered my original question: Why are you here? You hate Sylvana, so I know it's not just to warn me."

"Isn't it obvious?" Eden asked. "If I'm right, that means we're on the same side now. Our friends are in the same place, being held captive by the same person. And it's up to us to save them."

Violet stared at her for another moment. Finally she nodded, making the bun on top of her head bounce. "Okay. Let's do it." And, unbelievably, Violet and Eden shook hands in agreement.

"I don't think we should try this alone," Violet said. "We can ask some of the other Electric to help. But it might be tough to get them on board."

Eden understood that. She wouldn't have wanted to team up with them either, if there'd been any other option.

"Where are they, anyway?"

"Most of them went to a party after the auction."

"But not you?"

Violet wrinkled her nose. "I wasn't in the mood.

Hey," she said. "Heloise left during the auction too. After Brightly and Sylvana, but before the sale was over. Do you think Brightly's got her too?"

"Could be," Eden said.

"We'd better figure out what to do. Where do we start?"

Eden thought about how the Loyals had planned their mission. "We should use any resources we have," she said. "Do any of the Electric have powers that could help us?"

"Absolutely," Violet said. "Sylvana recruits based on powers."

Tyler leaned forward with interest. He was in for a pretty intense look at the genie alumni's world of magic. Eden hoped he could handle it.

"Okay," Eden said. "What have we got?"

"Well, Monroe wished for super strength, and to need no sleep."

"So she's like a vampire."

Violet laughed. "Basically. Except she doesn't drink blood. I don't think."

"What about Athena?"

"Athena wished to remember everything. She'll never forget a single fact or memory."

"A perfect brain. That's a good one," Eden admitted.

"Julianna might have been useful," Violet said. "She can change states of matter with a touch—so she can turn walls into gas and walk through them, turn a glass of water into ice—"

"Make plasma into gas?" Eden exclaimed. "Violet, that's perfect!"

"But she's not here," Violet said. "She left for Japan this morning."

"Oh." Eden was crestfallen—but she kept thinking. "What about Kingsley?"

Violet stretched out her hands to inspect her fingernails. "Kingsley wished for beautiful things to fall at her feet. She couldn't escape a life of luxury if she tried. Not that she's trying."

"I'm assuming the lamp doesn't count as a beautiful thing?"

"Nice try, but I'm pretty sure Sylvana gave that a shot early on."

Eden cleared her throat. "Just out of curiosity, what power does Sylvana have?"

"Isn't it obvious?" Violet's deep-brown eyes met Eden's. "The power of persuasion. Uncanny control over minds."

"Mortals' minds?"

"Mortal, immortal, animal, vegetable, mineral, you name it. No one can resist her."

In a way, of course, Eden *had* known it. She'd seen Sylvana sweep everyone off their feet, from the cops in San Diego to the Rockwells' father.

It wasn't just her beauty or charisma. There was something supernatural about it.

Eden had even felt it herself when they'd gazed out at the Pacific Ocean from a hot-air balloon in San Diego. Eventually she'd managed to see the truth, but perhaps that was only because of the bracelet's protection. Brightly had needed help to see past Sylvana's lies, too—and he'd gotten it through his Veritas.

"Hold on," Tyler said. Both Eden and Violet turned to him in surprise. "Sorry to interrupt, but I've got to get this straight. All of you Electric know that she has this power of persuasion, but you still commit your lives to her cause anyway?"

Violet looked at the floor. "I think we all have our own reasons for being part of Electra." Her eyes lifted, and in them, Eden saw a spark of something new. "But to be honest, I've started to ask myself the same thing."

"What about Heloise?" Eden asked. "Does she have any powers?"

Violet clicked her tongue. "You know, I'm not sure. "She only rejoined Electra a year ago. She used to be Electric, but then she disappeared for about a hundred years."

"Disappeared? Why?"

"Apparently she and Sylvana had some kind of falling-out. But they're best friends now." Violet rolled her eyes, giving Eden the feeling there was more to the story.

That left only one other member of Electra that Eden could think of. "What about you?"

Violet seemed to shrink an inch or two. She looked down at the coffee table. "I don't have any powers," she said apologetically. "I didn't make my thousandth wish wisely. So I'm not as valuable as most of the others."

That was a weird way to put it, Eden thought. "Well, think how valuable you'll be when you're leading the charge to save Sylvana."

Just then, Violet's cell phone rang. She snatched it up.

"*Bonsoir*, Athena." She paused for a moment. "No, I haven't heard from her either. Have you tried calling her?" Her lips pursed as she listened. "Look, I think you should come to my room. I want to show you something." She paused. "You've got to see for yourself. Trust me. This is"—her eyes drifted to Eden—"important."

Twenty-Six

Violet wanted Eden and Tyler to wait on the balcony. That way she could explain the situation to the Electric before the women saw them.

This wasn't one of the balconies with the red geraniums facing Avenue Montaigne, but a larger one, facing west. When Violet moved the dark-green curtains aside, Eden couldn't understand why they'd ever been closed. Through the sliding glass door was a clear view of the Eiffel Tower.

"Violet!" Eden said as they stepped out into the crisp night air. She rushed to the black iron railing at the edge. "It's *spectacular*."

Beside her, Tyler whistled low.

Orangey-gold lights lit up the *Tour Eiffel*, making it glow against the stark night sky. Naturally, Eden had pored over photos of it back in the lesson room of the lamp, and she'd seen it from afar a few times yesterday.

In daylight, it was a silver-brown sentry staunchly straddling a grassy field. At night, incandescent as it was now, it presided over Paris like a prince.

"It is special, isn't it?" Violet said as she came up to join them. "I was here when they unveiled it for the World's Fair, in 1889. Trust me, not everyone was a fan at first."

"You were *there*?" Tyler asked in awe. Violet looked at him, shrugged, and nodded. Eden supposed she'd accepted the fact that he knew most of their secrets by now.

"I remember learning about that," Eden said. This, like everything else, Xavier had covered in lessons. "There was a committee formed to protest its construction."

"That's right," Violet said. "Thank goodness Mr. Eiffel didn't listen."

Just then, a knock came at the door.

"Here they are," Violet said, seeming nervous suddenly. "Now remember, don't come in. I'll come out and get you once they've digested the idea."

"Got it," Eden said.

Violet went inside and closed the curtains behind her. Eden and Tyler remained outside.

"Wow," Tyler said. "The Eiffel Tower. I never really thought I'd get to see it."

"I know what you mean," Eden said.

Tyler turned to her. "So you're on Earth for good. Right?"

"Yeah," she said. "In New York, with a genie alum named Pepper. She's so cool." When Eden thought about Pepper, a weird lump rose in her throat. "Hopefully you'll meet her tonight—when we get her back from Brightly."

"Eden," Tyler said, "that's *amazing*. You're living the life you dreamed about."

When she thought about it that way, she had to smile. "I guess you're right," she said.

"I just wish you lived in California." Tyler grinned, showing those crooked teeth again. "Think you guys would ever move?"

Right at that moment, the Eiffel Tower began to glitter with white lights. Eden clapped her hands together as they danced from its base to its pinnacle.

"Tyler!" she said. "Isn't it beautiful?"

"Yep," he said. But he was facing her, not the lights.

Eden stared dreamily as it sparkled. She didn't know whether this was a special event, or something that happened all the time—but either way, it had to be a good sign.

"Here she is!" Kingsley roared as she ripped the curtains open. She looked like even more of a princess than usual, in a mermaid-style peacock-blue gown.

She yanked the sliding door aside and barged through. Behind her were Athena and Monroe.

Eden's magic feeling dissolved instantly. Maybe she'd been overly optimistic—because the Electric did not seem interested in joining forces.

"Get in here, you little brat," Monroe snarled as she yanked Eden off the balcony. Like Kingsley, she was also wearing a gown. Hers was lacy, black, and off the shoulder.

"Bring her to the bedroom!" Athena shouted, leading the way.

Monroe picked Eden up with one hand and flung her onto the bed in the other room. It took her no more effort than sending a paper airplane on its way. A few seconds later, Tyler crash-landed on the bed too.

"Violet, what were you thinking?" Kingsley yelled. "You left them out on the balcony? She could have escaped!"

"Why would she do that? She came to *me*!" In her bathrobe and topknot, Violet looked frumpy and flustered compared to the others.

"Well, she's not going anywhere now," Monroe growled. She bared a mouthful of teeth that Eden would swear looked abnormally sharp.

"Violet, you're so *gullible*," Athena said scornfully.

Kingsley stabbed a finger at Eden. "What have you done to Sylvana?"

"Nothing!"

"Why do you want us to go to Brightly Tech?"

Eden scooted up on the bed and leaned back on the pillows. Next to her, Tyler did the same. The Electric had surrounded them.

"This is crazy," Eden protested. "My friends are being held by Brightly, and I happen to know that Sylvana is too. I thought we could team up and go rescue them." She crossed her arms angrily. "Apparently I was wrong."

"You can say that again," Kingsley snapped. "*Dead* wrong, to think we'd fall for a stupid story like that. And now the two of you are going to stay here until Sylvana gets back."

"But she's not *going* to!" Eden exclaimed. "Don't you understand?"

"Unfortunately for you," Athena said, "Violet's the only one here who's dumb enough to believe you."

Violet's eyes sparked with indignation. "Fine," she said. "Maybe I'm wrong. But what if I'm not?"

They rolled their eyes.

"We've all been trying to get in touch with Sylvana. But has anyone heard from her?"

They all checked their phones. "Not yet," Monroe murmured.

"Doesn't that seem strange?" Violet said. "We all saw her leave the auction with Brightly, so it's safe to assume she's still with him. Why wouldn't she be answering her phone unless something was wrong?"

Kingsley, Athena, and Monroe looked at each other and shrugged.

"Think about it. What if she *is* in trouble, and we're sitting here doing nothing about it?"

"What about Heloise?" Athena asked. "She left the auction early too, but I didn't see her at the party. Has anyone spoken to her?"

The others shook their heads. Athena pulled out her phone and dialed.

"Heloise!" Athena left the bedroom to talk to her.

Kingsley glowered at Eden. "How'd you make it to this hotel without being caught?" she asked. "All of Paris is searching for you."

"She was wearing a wig," Violet said.

Kingsley snorted. "Mortals. Their stupidity baffles me more every day."

"Why are *you* here?" Monroe asked Tyler in her low, raspy voice.

Tyler cleared his throat. "I came to help Eden," he said.

The alumni groaned. "Thirteen-year-old mortal to the rescue," Kingsley chided. "Nice try, Romeo."

Eden was mortified. Tyler had come all the way to Paris only to wind up at the mercy of the same cruel women who'd terrorized his family in San Diego.

Athena reentered the bedroom triumphantly. "Everything's fine," she announced. "Heloise is with Sylvana." She glanced at Eden. "The girl was right— they're at Brightly Tech. And the lamp is there too." A smirk crept across her face. "Lucky for us, we've got the last piece of the puzzle. Now we just need to get her there."

Eden closed her eyes in dismay. She'd messed up again! She'd gambled on the plans she'd overheard Brightly making, thinking he wouldn't fall victim to Sylvana's charms again. But she must have underestimated Sylvana's power of persuasion. It seemed she really was unstoppable.

"Everything's going according to plan!" Kingsley cackled.

"Even better than we planned," Athena said with relish.

It was infuriating: Eden had played right into their horrible hands. She'd wanted to fix everything, but just like when she'd been invisible in Brightly Tech, she'd made the wrong decision. This time, she'd really made a mess of things. She'd let down everyone she cared about: not only Pepper and the Loyals, who she had no hope of rescuing now, but also her masters, who were still stuck in the lamp, blind and helpless, and Tyler, who'd spent all of his and Sasha's savings to come here.

She couldn't seem to do the right thing. Lately, it seemed like there was no point even trying.

"Put some clothes on, Violet," said Athena. "We need to get to Brightly Tech."

Twenty-Seven

It was nearly midnight when they arrived at Brightly Tech. The lights were off, and all the employees were long gone. Anyone looking at the building would think it was vacant.

"Heloise said the door on the far right is open," said Athena, leading the way.

The Electric had put the wig on Eden again so they could smuggle her out of the hotel. They'd also left Tyler behind. Thinking about him standing on the sidewalk outside made Eden sick with sadness.

Gripping Eden by the arms, Monroe and Kingsley dragged her across the lobby and onto an elevator. After witnessing Monroe's supernatural strength in action, Eden knew there was no use trying to break free.

Athena pressed the button for the eighth floor. When they reached it, she had no trouble opening the door behind the reception desk, even without an ID card.

They crossed into the room with the wood-paneled walls. The fish tank glowed softly, providing the only muted light.

"No one's here," Eden said. "You sure you know where you're going?"

Athena shot her a malicious glare. "They're here, don't you worry."

Monroe squeezed her arm so tightly, it felt like she might crush the bone.

"*Ow,*" Eden squealed. "Geez!"

They followed Athena through the door on the right into Brightly's office. In addition to his massive desk were a foosball table, a few arcade-style game machines, and a leather sofa that faced a gigantic television screen. On the walls were autographed photos, guitars, and sports jerseys.

Athena led them to a tall display case on the far wall. It was filled with tiny soldiers, model airplanes, and small brawny figures in colorful costumes. She opened the glass door, then reached toward a muscular figurine with a black cape and a black mask. She pressed a button on his stomach.

"To the bat cave," the figurine growled. And with that, the display case slid aside to reveal a white staircase.

Eden's eyes widened. *Here* was the way to the ninth

floor. Even if she'd spent hours exploring Brightly Tech, she never would have discovered this.

At the top of the stairs was the bright white hallway Eden had seen two nights earlier. "Second door," said Athena, walking past the first door they came to. She opened the next one and held it open while Monroe walked through, pulling Eden by the wrist. Kingsley and Violet were close behind.

Like before, the lab was dark. Only the purple light of the plasma shield glowed from the middle of the room.

"Who's there?" someone cried as they walked in. *"Help!"*

Behind them, the door slammed shut.

Sensing danger, Eden squinted in the dark.

A little more than halfway down the wall next to them was a figure with long dreads: Bola. She was standing with her back flush against the wall.

Eden hooked her head around to see beyond Bola. Was that Pepper behind her?

"What—" Eden began—but in the next instant, the breath was sucked out of her as her own body slammed against the wall.

She screamed, but the sound was lost in the chorus of cries from all the others.

"What the—?" Kingsley gasped from behind her.

In front of Eden, Monroe had managed to keep

herself a foot away from the wall, and was trying her hardest to flee. But the force overcame even her super-natural strength, and she slammed against the wall too. She howled in agony—more likely from the sting of defeat than any physical pain.

The others had probably never experienced any-thing like this—but Eden had. The same inconceivably strong magnetic force that had pinned her to the chair was now pinning them to the wall.

They'd walked directly into a trap.

"Eden, is that you?" came Pepper's voice. Despite the circumstances, hearing that lovely, melodic voice gave Eden a surge of joy.

"Pepper!" Eden cried. "Is Delta there too?"

"Over here," said Delta. Her voice was muffled. "Face-first against the wall."

"Pepper, I'm sorry about before!" Eden said. Nor-mally she would have been embarrassed to say it in front of the Electric, but now she didn't care. "I'm so sorry. I love you!"

"No, *I'm* sorry!" Pepper said. "I never meant to make you feel that way. I love you too!"

"Shut *up*!" Kingsley yelled.

"What's going on?" came Athena's voice from the far left. She'd held the door open for the rest of them, so she would have been the last one to enter. If she was stuck to the wall, that meant none of them had escaped.

"Where's Sylvana?" Kingsley screeched.

"Over here." Sylvana's voice came from the very back of the room, past Pepper and the Loyals. "And to think, I thought you all were here to rescue me."

"What do you mean?" Kingsley cried. "Can't you tell Brightly to let us go?"

"I'm stuck here just like you," Sylvana growled.

"But Heloise said everything was fine!" Athena said.

"What are you talking about?" Sylvana roared. "Heloise isn't here!"

"She's not?"

"No!"

"But—"

"He tricked us all!" Sylvana said bitterly. "And now we're all trapped here together."

"He *did*?" Kingsley asked.

"Yes, I suppose I did." Brightly's cane clicked on the floor as he limped out from the shadows. Evidently he'd been watching from the other side of the lab. Since the back of Eden's head was stuck to the wall, she had a clear view of him, decked out in a black suit with a bow tie.

Her eyes had adjusted to the dark, so now she could make out more of the lab. In the dim half-light, she saw Jane Johnston near the lamp's purple glow. As usual, she was holding a Brightly tablet. It seemed to be permanently connected to her hand. Eden didn't see Jean Luc or Dr. Evans, but she did see the damage from the fire she'd caused among the oxygen tanks (which were, of course, no longer there). She could also see that the section of wall she'd cut with the laser had been sloppily patched up.

Eden gritted her teeth. With all her might, she wished she had a laser in her hand now. Too bad she wasn't the one with wishes to make.

"Look at y'all, caught like little flies on sticky flypaper." Brightly giggled in glee as he limped past them. "I thought I was lucky to get four, and then five more showed up!"

Eden noticed that he stayed about six feet away from the wall, behind a line of electrical tape on the floor that ran parallel to it. Her guess was that it indicated the reach of the magnetic force.

"What do you think you're doing?" Athena thundered.

"Since you asked," Brightly said, "I'll tell you. I'm an honest guy—well, when I can be." He smiled that big horsey smile. "I'm going to siphon every little secret about that lamp from your brains. And if you try to lie to me, I'll know it—thanks to my Veritas."

"Your *what*?" Athena hissed.

"The thing I told you about!" Eden said. "I saw it when I spied on him and Sylvana."

"Excuse me—what?" Sylvana said. "You *spied* on us?"

"What if we won't tell you anything?" said Kingsley defiantly.

"Then you can forget about gettin' off that wall," Brightly said. "Only a few of my most trusted employees know that this lab exists. We can keep you here for weeks. However long it takes till I get what I want."

"Ha!" Bola spat. "Weeks are nothing to us. We'll wait for decades."

"Is that right!" Brightly said, grinning. "Well, I don't think it's going to take that long. Sylvana here told me over lunch today that she knows how to get all the power in that genie lamp." He limped over to stand in front of Sylvana. "I kept my end of the bargain. Now that you've seen the lamp, it's time for you to spill—just like we discussed. Except I don't think we'll be partners after all."

"David, darling," Sylvana said. "You're making a mistake." Her tone was light, but it sounded forced—as if she were straining to keep her composure.

"I disagree," Brightly said. "Seems to me, the mistake would have been listenin' to you. You're used to people believin' all your lies. But that's about to end."

"You can't do this without me!" she said. "You *need* me!"

"*Need* you?" Brightly hobbled back down the line of alumni. "I don't need anybody! I built this company all by myself!"

Sylvana began to laugh a low, menacing chuckle.

"What are you *laughin'* at?"

"You're nothing but a boy," she said. "A boy with a

lot of toys, and a secret lair full of science experiments that you get to by pushing a button on your little action figure."

Brightly's face had gone crimson. "A *boy*? I'm the most powerful man in the world!" All traces of the humility he'd tried to feign were gone.

"You're dreaming!" Sylvana yelled. "You'll never be as powerful as *me*!"

Fuming, Brightly limped over and stopped in front of Eden.

"I'm ready for my first wish!" He shot a finger toward Sylvana. "I wish that *that woman* would never be able to tell another lie—or withhold any little bit of the truth!"

Eden's jaw dropped open. She despised Brightly, but his wish was absolutely brilliant.

The force holding her to the wall wouldn't allow her to snap her fingers, but she could see light shine through the letters on her genie bracelet as the magical transaction took place.

Every person in the room stayed silent, awaiting Sylvana's next words.

"I—I—" she sputtered.

"Well?" Brightly prompted. "Tell the truth. Were you goin' to use me?"

"*Yes!*" said Sylvana. "I thought I could manipulate you like I manipulate everyone else!"

Next to Eden, Kingsley gasped.

"Is that right?" Brightly smirked. He indicated the other alumni. "Does that include these other ladies stuck up on the sticky flypaper wall?"

"Yes!"

"Hold up. Ex*cuse* me?" said Athena.

"Yeah, *what*?" Kingsley chimed in.

"All this time they've been working for *me*, to help *me* get the lamp's power!" Sylvana cried. "Once I learned that you'd gotten ahold of the lamp, I thought I could finally get what I want!"

"Well, well. That didn't work out the way you planned, did it?" Brightly taunted.

"No!"

Although it was satisfying to hear Sylvana speak the truth, Eden knew that Brightly's wish had made their situation much more precarious. Before, there was no chance Sylvana would have told Brightly what he wanted to know. Now, she had no choice.

As soon as he finished teasing her and got down to business, he was going to ask how to get the lamp's power. And Sylvana would tell him the key was getting the bracelet off the resident genie. Eden still didn't even know what made the bracelet come off—but if Brightly asked, Sylvana would explain it.

It was bad enough that if Brightly were to take the lamp's power, he'd have the world at his horrible fingertips. But even worse, its current masters would cease to exist. Xavier and Goldie had raised Eden, loved her, and changed the lamp's rules to let her live free on Earth. She simply couldn't let them lose their lives.

Even though she couldn't move, she had to take action.

"Monroe!" she whispered. She couldn't move her head, but she knew Monroe was close on her right side.

"Yeah," Monroe answered low.

"I saw you trying to get away from the wall. You almost had it. If you focused, do you think you could pull yourself off?"

"Maybe," Monroe said. "But it would be hard."

Brightly was too busy ridiculing Sylvana to notice that Eden and Monroe were talking.

"Do you see the line on the floor that he's standing behind?" Eden asked. "I think that's the threshold. If he stays on that side, the magnetic force can't reach him."

"Yeah," Monroe said.

"Okay. Bola's on your other side, right?"

Out of the corner of her eye, Eden saw Monroe move her head slightly to see. The constraints of normal human strength made even that much movement impossible for Eden.

"Yeah," rasped Monroe.

"Do you think you could pull her off the wall and throw her across the threshold?"

Monroe was silent for a moment. Then:

"Nah. I hate Bola."

Eden gritted her teeth in frustration. "I understand that. But she can't feel pain. If you could get her off the wall, she might be able to get the lamp out of the cage. I think she's the only one who could do it."

Monroe was silent for another few seconds.

"Monroe," Eden said, "if we don't stop Brightly, he's going to take the lamp's power for himself. That would be bad for *all* of us."

"What's going on over here?" Jane had strolled up to stand in front of Eden, right behind the line of tape.

Brightly hobbled over to stand with her. He sized Eden up, leaning on his cane. "Hey, little genie. You causin' trouble again?"

Eden's heart pounded in her chest.

"Did you see all the damage you did to my lab?" He lifted his cane and shook it at her. "And what about my leg? You gave me second-degree burns!"

"Well, you'd been torturing me for hours!" Eden fired back.

"*Torturin'* you?" He chuckled. "That's a little dramatic, don't ya think? We were merely performing tests on a subject."

"I'm not a subject for your lab experiments. I'm a *person*!"

"Tell him, Eden!" Pepper whooped.

"You are a *genie*," Brightly pronounced disdainfully.

"Yes!" Eden said. "A *person* who's a genie."

"David," Jane said, "remember what we're here for."

Brightly turned from Eden and limped back over to Sylvana. Eden's heart fell. Accidentally getting his attention was the best thing she'd done yet. By distracting him, she'd held him off for a few moments.

Too bad Jane was too levelheaded for that to work for long. Brightly was a loose cannon, but Jane always calmed him down and kept him on task.

"Today you told me that you know how to get the lamp's power," Brightly said to Sylvana. "Is that true?"

"Yes," said Sylvana. It sounded like she was speaking through gritted teeth.

Brightly looked over at Jane, who was watching the tablet—confirming that Brightly's wish had achieved its purpose, Eden supposed. She nodded at Brightly.

Eden's mind was spinning. What could she do to distract him?

"Whoo!" Brightly hooted. He rubbed his hands together. "Spill it, sister. How do I get that genie lamp power for myself?"

Like a flash, an idea hit Eden. It was simple, but it just might work.

"I'm SIIIINGIN' in the rain!" she sang out as loud as she could.

Brightly and Jane whipped around to face her. Both of them looked absolutely baffled.

"Just SIIIINGIN' in the rain!"

Pepper's beautiful voice was the next to join: "What a glorious feeling, I'm happy again!"

"Why are y'all *singin'*?" Brightly demanded.

"Seriously," Kingsley snapped.

Bola caught on next.

"Happy birthday to you," she sang over top of them. "Happy birthday to you!"

"David, ask the question again!" Jane urged. For once, she was getting flustered too.

"Why in the world are they *singin'*?" Brightly asked again.

"They're trying to drown her out!"

Any of the alumni who hadn't understood the purpose of the singing before did now. Every voice joined in, resulting in a loud, chaotic cacophony. A Christmas carol came from one end; "Twinkle, Twinkle, Little Star" came from the other. Next to Eden, Monroe made a terrible siren sound.

Jane had finally slipped up—and judging by the look on her face, she knew it. In trying to clue Brightly in, she'd unwittingly helped the alumni.

Even if Sylvana were to tell Brightly precisely what

he wanted to know, there was no chance he'd be able to hear it now.

"Quiet!!" Brightly screamed. "I need quiet!"

But instead, a new voice joined in.

"Eden!" it called from the other side of the lab. "Are you here?"

Eden's heart nearly leaped across the room to where he was.

He'd shown up. *Again*, he'd shown up.

"Tyler!" she yelled. "I'm here!"

Brightly whipped around. "Who's that?" He hobbled forward a little.

The alumni's cacophony quieted as some of them stopped making noise.

"Eden! Are you okay?" Tyler asked, coming closer.

"Stay back!" Eden warned. "I'm fine, I just can't move."

He'd come in through the door on the opposite side of the room—the one Athena had been instructed to walk past. Because of that, he'd avoided Brightly's trap. As he moved forward cautiously, Eden could see that he was brandishing a fancy-looking guitar.

"Is that *my* guitar you're holdin'?" Brightly asked in disbelief.

Tyler held it over his head. "Elvis Presley's 1942 Martin D-18. That's what the plaque below it said." Eden could tell he was afraid, but he didn't back down.

He held it high above the edge of a lab table. "If you don't let Eden and her friends come with me right now, I'm going to smash it into splinters."

"Stop him, Jane!" Brightly shrieked. "That belonged to the King!"

"David, calm down!" Jane scolded. She narrowed her eyes at Tyler and started stalking toward him. "How did you get in here?"

It was as if Tyler had read Eden's mind: he'd provided the perfect distraction. Brightly and Jane were both so focused on him that they missed the moment when Monroe took action. She reached out, peeled Bola off the wall, and launched her across the threshold like a human cannonball. Bola flew through the air and landed on Brightly's back, knocking him to the floor.

He screamed at a pitch so high, it made Eden's ears ring. "My leg!" he wailed.

Bola reached down and scooped him up from under the arms. Groaning with effort, she lifted him, turned him toward the wall, and shoved him across the line of tape. Brightly went flying face-first into the space she'd vacated on the wall.

Eden watched in awe. Bola was truly a force to be reckoned with.

"JANE!!!" Brightly roared from his spread-eagled position. "Help me!!"

Unlike Brightly, Bola didn't waste a second gloating.

She rushed to the lamp, aglow in purple in its cage on the lab table, and stuck her hands inside. Eden cringed, remembering the excruciating pain that had ripped through her when she'd touched the plasma. Even knowing that Bola was immune to pain, Eden was shocked to see that she really didn't appear to feel a thing.

However, the bars of the cage were too close together for her to remove the lamp. She tried to pull them apart, but they wouldn't budge.

"Help!!" Brightly screamed. Eden was glad that his face was plastered against the wall so he couldn't see Bola struggling with the bars.

Next to Eden, a second figure sprang forward lithely. Monroe had launched herself off the wall too.

She stepped up to the cage encasing the lamp and placed her own hands on the metal. As she pried the bars apart, she let out a bloodcurdling scream. She might have supernatural strength, but unlike Bola, she still felt pain. The circumference of that ball of plasma, as blisteringly hot as the surface of the sun, would be burning her fingers with a vengeance.

But after a few moments, it was done. Monroe staggered aside, and Bola reached in and pulled the lamp free.

From the first time she'd seen her in the flesh, Eden had thought Bola looked like a champion. Now, as she lifted the lamp high above her head like a trophy, that vision was gloriously manifested. Cheers erupted down the line of alumni.

"Now I need to make a request for reentry!" Eden said.

But she was interrupted by a loud crack. She squeezed her eyes shut as bright light filled the lab.

"What happened?" Brightly whimpered.

When Eden opened her eyes, her heart soared. All at once, she knew everything would be all right. Because standing next to Bola was one of the masters of the lamp.

Twenty-Eight

Goldie was as pretty and pink-cheeked as ever, but Eden had never seen her look quite so ferocious. Her eyes glittered as they swept over the lab.

"What in heaven's name is going on here?" she demanded.

"There's a magnetic force keeping us stuck us to this wall!" Eden said.

Goldie snapped her fingers, and Eden dropped to the floor. She stretched her arms and rotated her ankles. It was good to be able to move again.

Looking down the line, she saw that Pepper and Delta had been released too—but not Brightly or the Electric.

Eden rushed to her master. "Goldie!"

"My darling girl," said Goldie warmly.

Eden hugged her tightly. They'd only been apart for a few weeks, but it felt like years.

When they parted, Pepper was beside them, beaming as brilliantly as ever. "Phew," she said. "What a wild ride, kid!"

"Pepper!" Eden wrapped her arms around her guardian too.

While Goldie greeted the other Loyals, Eden spotted Tyler, looking slightly stunned, standing by a lab table where he'd set the (still intact) guitar.

"Tyler!" she said, running to him. "You're *amazing*. How'd you find us?"

He shrugged shyly. "Getting to Brightly Tech was easy enough. Then I kept finding open doors, so I figured I was on the right track. When I got to Brightly's office, that display case had been moved aside to show the stairs, and I heard voices coming from up there."

"Who's this young man?" Goldie asked, appearing beside them.

"This is my friend Tyler," said Eden.

"Nice to meet you." Tyler's smile showed his crooked teeth.

Goldie's eyes lit up incredulously. "From San Diego?"

"He came here to help me," said Eden.

"You dear boy!" Goldie looked overcome with happiness. She took the sides of Tyler's head affectionately and gave him a big kiss on the cheek.

"This is all very sweet," Kingsley snapped. Now

Eden could see the ungainly position she'd been caught in, with her arms sticking out at weird angles. "But some of us are still *stuck* on a *wall* over here."

Goldie smoothed a few stray hairs from her silver-blond bun. "Yes, what about you. . . . What do you call yourselves? *Electric*. How did you end up here?"

"I came here for the lamp, but Brightly tricked me and trapped me," Sylvana said bitterly. "Of course, I was trying to get its power for myself."

"Well, that's nothing new, is it?" Goldie said. But then she balked. "Wait a second. Did you really just tell the truth about that?"

Sylvana sighed. "I have no choice anymore. Brightly wished that I could never tell another lie."

Goldie crossed her arms and smiled. "Well, isn't that interesting."

"Hello! Can y'all *please* let me down now? I still have two more wishes to make!" Having his face mashed into the wall made Brightly's words a little muffled.

"Ha!" Bola laughed harshly. "You *really* think you get to make more wishes *now*?" She shook her head and clicked her tongue.

"Why wouldn't I?" Brightly yelled into the wall.

"Is he *serious*?" murmured Pepper.

"You'd better let me free this instant," Brightly shouted. "This is *my* lab!"

"Oh, Mr. Brightly. We have things to discuss before that happens," said Goldie, striding toward him.

"You won't get away with this," Brightly said viciously. "My employees will be here to help me any minute."

"Really?" said Eden. "I haven't seen Jean Luc or Dr. Evans since we arrived."

"Well, where's *Jane*?" he cried.

"She's gone too," said Pepper. "She must have snuck out the back door."

That shut him up—but not for long. "Doesn't matter," he growled. "I don't need anyone!"

"Clearly," Delta quipped. Pepper and Eden looked at each other and giggled.

"Ex*cuse* me!" Eden could tell Brightly was heading for a tantrum. "Do you even know who I *am*?"

"Sure we do," said Goldie calmly. "You're the man who stole the lamp."

"I'm the founder of Brightly Tech," Brightly crowed. "The most powerful man in the world!"

"Oh, my! Is that right?" Goldie cooed. "Why don't you use some of that power to look at me when I'm talking to you?"

"I can't," he yelled. "I'm stuck like this!"

Goldie held out her hand and snapped, and instantly Brightly's back slammed against the wall, whipping him around to face the room.

"That's better," she said. "Hello, Mr. Brightly."

Looking at him straight on, Eden could see that both of Brightly's glasses lenses were shattered—and also, that he looked absolutely terrified.

"Who *are* you?" he asked with a quaver in his voice.

Goldie put her hands on her hips. "I'm one of the masters of the lamp. And I'm here to tell you that this granting is officially over."

"What?" Brightly squawked. "I don't get my other wishes?"

"No, sir. And I'll thank you to never use that tone of voice in my presence again." Goldie shook her head. "You're a grown man. Why don't you start acting like it?"

Brightly huffed.

"Eden," said Goldie, "did Mr. Brightly block the telescope?"

"Yep. He put a plasma shield over the lamp."

Goldie's eyes flashed. "A *what*?"

"Sort of like a force field," Eden explained. "That's why messages couldn't go in and out, and I couldn't make a request for reentry."

Goldie's cheeks flushed a deeper shade of pink. "Well, I *never*."

Pepper put an arm around Eden. "When Brightly summoned Eden, he put the plasma shield on the lamp and held her here so he could do tests on her." Her nose crinkled in disgust. "Luckily, she escaped. But then Brightly had all of Paris searching for her. He said she was his daughter, and that she'd been kidnapped. He even offered a reward."

Goldie narrowed her eyes at Brightly. "You should be ashamed of yourself," she scolded. Then to Eden: "How did you get the lamp free?"

"Bola did it!" Eden said. "Monroe used her super strength to separate the cage's bars, and then Bola reached into the plasma and pulled it free. They were amazing!"

"A Loyal and an Electric, working together," Goldie said with amusement. "Who would have guessed it." Bola raised her eyebrows at Monroe, who, for a split second, looked like she might actually smile—but then they turned away from each other awkwardly.

Goldie's attention returned to Brightly. "Listen closely, Mr. Brightly. First thing in the morning, you're going to tell the press that the search was a hoax. You won't give any additional information, and you'll never speak to anyone about it again. Do you understand?"

"Fine," Brightly grumbled.

"I beg your pardon." Goldie seemed to grow an inch taller. "Do you understand?"

"I understand," he said in defeat.

Goldie glowered at him. "You're going to stay far away from this lamp and these women for the rest of your pitiful life. And you're never to tell a soul what you know about the lamp. Do you understand?"

"I understand." Maybe it was true that Brightly was one of the world's most powerful people, but at the moment, he was as deflated as a popped balloon.

Goldie walked right up to the wall and grabbed his collar. Apparently, the magnetism's pull was no match for the power of a master of the lamp. "If you don't follow these instructions *precisely*, you're going to wish you never even heard the word *genie*. Do you understand me?"

"Yes, ma'am," Brightly said meekly. "May I go home now?"

Goldie snapped her fingers, and he dropped to his feet. He rubbed the side of his face that had been stuck to the wall.

"Tyler," Goldie said, "could you be a dear and escort Mr. Brightly out of the building?"

Tyler stood up a little straighter. "No problem."

"Thank you, love. Goodbye, Mr. Brightly." Scowling, Brightly stooped to pick his cane up off the floor; then Tyler took his arm and led him out.

With Brightly gone, all eyes turned to the remaining Electra members on the wall: Violet, Kingsley, Athena, and Sylvana.

you since the beginning, almost. But you always treated me like I was second-rate."

"What do you *mean*?" Sylvana protested. "I—" But she couldn't seem to get the words out. It was as if she were physically choking on her lie. In its place, the truth came rushing out: "I know."

Violet nodded. "I need to remember that there are other things out there in the world. Good things." She threw her shoulders back. "I officially resign."

Eden had to suppress a cheer. She still didn't care for the other Electric, but she'd developed a soft spot for Violet.

Sylvana's honey-colored hair had gone limp, and her lipstick was smeared. Standing alone against the wall, she was a smaller, more pitiful version of her former self.

"But what will I *do*?" she said softly.

"You could keep Electra operating," Goldie suggested. "Run it as a normal auction house."

Sylvana sniffed.

"Sylvana, let me tell you something," Goldie said. "Actually, this goes for all of you." The eyes of every genie alum turned to her—Electric and Loyal. "Some of you have represented this legacy poorly. Some of you have been devious and vengeful. Some of you have even removed your genie bracelets." She paused for a moment and closed her eyes. That one seemed to hurt her the most. "But. You are still genie alumni. And do you know what that means?"

Eden smiled. She knew exactly what was coming.

"Each and every one of you is graceful, brilliant, and terribly beautiful."

Eden looked at Violet, in jeans, a T-shirt, and a floppy topknot.

Then at Monroe, who, for once, was staring soberly rather than scowling.

At Kingsley, in her blue mermaid dress.

At Delta, with her huge eyes, frizzy hair, and the gap between her teeth.

And the others: Bola, Pepper, and Sylvana.

Each of them was a part of this legacy, too.

"Don't you ever, *ever* forget that," said Goldie.

Pepper put her arm around Eden's shoulders and gave her a squeeze.

"Now then! What do you say we carry on with our lives?" Goldie sniffed. "I'm going to turn into a pumpkin soon."

The former Electric started trickling out, though some of them stopped to say goodbye to Goldie first. As the last one made her exit, Goldie's eyes settled on Eden and Pepper. "Not you two, of course. I promised Xavier he could do the post-granting assessment. As soon as I'm back in the lamp, he'll be on his way."

"That didn't cover it?" Eden asked.

"Of course not! This is Xavier we're talking about." Goldie's eyes twinkled. "Goodbye, my beauties!" She held the lamp out with the spout facing her, and there was a flash of light. When the lab faded to darkness again, she was gone.

Tyler came back through the door. "David Brightly has left the building," he announced. He looked around. "Where'd Goldie go?"

"Back in the lamp," Eden said. "But now—"

There was another flash of light. This one brought Xavier.

Even fresh out of the lamp, he was as elegant as ever. His dark hair was slicked back, his mustache was pencil-thin, and one eyebrow was raised coyly.

"Hello, Eden, Pepper," he greeted them. "Bola. Delta, good to see you. And . . ." His eyes rested on Tyler.

"Now," Eden said, "you get to meet Xavier."

Tyler approached him respectfully. "Hello, sir. It's an honor to meet you," he said.

Xavier raised his eyebrows at Eden. Pepper's grin couldn't have been any wider. "And you as well, my boy," he said. He took Tyler's outstretched hand and gave it a good, strong shake.

Xavier turned to Delta. "Delta, you have a house here in Paris, correct? Would you be so kind as to host us for a short meeting?"

"Sure," Delta said. Her eyes were massive as she nodded. "My car's parked outside."

"Very good." Xavier tugged at his mustache. "Now, what are the chances we could find a good Parisian baguette at this hour?"

Twenty-Nine

Delta's pets seemed to love Xavier almost as much as they loved Delta, so they swarmed the dinner table while the humans ate the bread and cheese they'd tracked down. Then, even though it was the middle of the night, Tyler and Bola joined Delta to take Trevor on a walk. Eden suspected that they were also trying to give her, Pepper, and Xavier privacy for the assessment.

Once they were alone, Eden and Pepper told him everything. It had turned into quite a story, and there were parts that Eden was nervous to tell. She expected him to scold her for setting the lab on fire, but she was wrong.

"That was quick thinking," he said. "You knew you had to get out of there, and you found a way to do it."

When she was done, he sat back in his chair and touched his fingertips together. "The world is changing," he said. "Much more rapidly than ever before. It seems technology on Earth has advanced to the point that it's nearly as powerful as the lamp's magic. In some ways, maybe it's even more powerful." He shook his head. "I've been remiss. I refused to acknowledge the importance of these advancements. I didn't equip you with the knowledge you needed."

Eden felt all mixed up. Hearing Xavier admit he was wrong was really disconcerting. "It all worked out in the end," she assured him.

"Yes, it did. And for that, we are fortunate." Xavier tugged on his moustache. "But we have to do better."

"What do we do?" Pepper asked.

"We adapt," he answered decisively. "Pepper, when you're back in New York, you must enroll Eden in a school with mortals. She's got to see what the world is truly like. No shielding her from it anymore."

A school with mortals. Eden swallowed. It was going to be different than Pepper's school of street smarts. But Xavier was right: it was time.

"Are you going to tell the other alumni that Eden is living on Earth?" Pepper asked.

Xavier pondered that. "I will if they ask," he said at last. "Although we wanted to keep it quiet, quite a few alumni know at this point. The others will most likely have seen Brightly's search for Eden in the news. Now that the spout is unsealed once again, I won't be surprised if questions come our way. And I won't lie to our genies."

"Xavier," Eden said, "do you really think Sylvana is done being evil?"

"It seems she doesn't have a choice," Xavier said. "She's lost her followers. And if she tells every person she meets that she wants to use them to find a genie lamp and take its power—well, I'd imagine it would be hard for her to find new ones."

"So is it safe to say Electra is no longer a threat?" Pepper asked hopefully.

"It seems to me that Electra may very well go on as a successful auction house. And in that, I wish Sylvana the best. I really do." Xavier smiled slyly. "I attended an auction there once, out of curiosity. I wore a big hat and sat in the back of the room. I must say, I was impressed."

Eden remembered how, in New York, she'd wondered whether Xavier had ever sat in on one of Pepper's shows. As she watched Pepper's lips curl up into a quiet smile, she had a hunch that Pepper was wondering the same thing. But neither of them asked. Some questions, Eden supposed, were better left unasked.

Just then, Delta, Bola, Tyler, and Trevor burst through the front door.

"Perfect timing," Xavier said. "Delta, you've been an excellent host, but I must return to the homestead."

Each of the women hugged him goodbye, and Tyler shook his hand.

"It seems my Eden has found some very good friends in you and your sister," Xavier said.

"She's been a very good friend to us," Tyler said.

Finally, it was Eden's turn to say goodbye.

"Until the next granting, my dear," said Xavier. "Whenever that may be. *Au revoir!*" With a salute and a flash of light, he was gone—and so was the lamp. Already, they were off to a new, unknown location somewhere on Earth.

It was sort of a relief to know that some things never changed.

Thirty

The next morning, not even the squawks and barks of Delta's menagerie could awaken Eden and Pepper. They slept past noon, and stirred only when the cat leapt onto the bed and nestled between them.

Pepper woke up giggling. "There's a cat in this house too?"

"Oh yeah. We met last night," Eden said, rubbing behind its ears to make it purr.

The cat must have crept through the splintery new hole in the door to their bedroom. Just as Eden had expected, Jane and Jean Luc had kicked it in after she'd escaped through the window.

A knock came at the door, followed by the sound of a throat being cleared.

"May I come in?" asked Bola.

Eden and Pepper glanced at each other with raised

eyebrows. Eden sat up straight and crossed her legs. "Sure."

Bola was dressed in black leather from head to toe, and her magenta lipstick had been freshly applied. "I've got to jet off," she said. "But first I want to say something." She took a few steps forward and sat stiffly at the foot of the bed. "I'm ... sorry." The words came out unnaturally, like this might be the first time she'd ever said them. "After yesterday's trip to Brightly Tech, I suppose I was a bit ... harsh."

Under the covers, Pepper squeezed Eden's hand.

Bola's eyebrows furrowed. "I'm not heartless, you know. In fact, I feel things very strongly. Perhaps that's why ..." She trailed off.

"You wanted to protect the lamp so badly?" Eden prompted.

"And *you*. I wanted to protect *you*," she said fiercely. Bola looked into Eden's eyes, and for the first time, Eden saw past her diamond-hard shell. She saw that beneath it was a sense of loyalty so strong, it took precedence over things that most people valued. Things like tact, and convention, and convenience.

Bola might not be Eden's favorite person now, or ever. But just like Pepper had promised, she *had* helped them. And Eden would never hesitate to trust her again.

"We never could have saved the lamp without you," Eden said. "I'm glad you came. I really mean that."

Bola's face softened. "Thank you for that," she said. For a moment Eden thought she was going to say more—or maybe, possibly, even hug her.

But neither of those things happened. She *was* still Bola, after all. In a flash, she was on her feet.

"I'll miss my flight if I dawdle any longer," she said. "Pepper, Eden. Until next time."

"Happy trails!" Pepper called behind her, waving. When Bola was gone, she turned to Eden. "Well!" she marveled. "What do you think of that?"

Once they were dressed, Pepper and Eden went downstairs to the living room, where Tyler had slept. He and Delta were playing with the pets—which included another dog and a few new birds. They seemed to multiply by the day.

"Sorry we slept so late," Eden said.

"That's okay," Tyler said. "I doubt I'll ever have another chance to play with pets that disappear and reappear." Another bird appeared to join the one already on his arm, and he laughed. Delta winked at Eden.

"We should probably leave today," Pepper said. "Unless you two want to stay in Paris longer?"

"I wish I could, but I should get back to San Diego," Tyler said. "I talked to my dad this morning. He's pretty mad. But he's glad you're okay, Eden."

"Do you have money to buy a flight?" Eden asked.

"We'll figure it out." Tyler shrugged and smiled. "He gave me a credit card number to use."

"Nonsense," said Pepper. "Your trip is on us."

"Oh, no. I couldn't—"

Pepper held up a hand to stop him. "Yes, you will! And also, the masters insist on flying you, your sister, and your father to New York to visit us—as soon as you're able."

"No way!" Tyler said, looking at Eden excitedly.

"Really, Pepper?" Eden was ecstatic.

"Of course! It seems Tyler made a very good impression on them." Pepper winked.

"I'd love to . . . but I don't know if my dad will go for that," Tyler said.

"Well, let's get him on the phone."

They set up a video chat like the one Brightly had used in the car when Eden was invisible. Eden got to talk to Sasha face-to-face, and Pepper got to meet both her and Mr. Rockwell. In California it was very early in the morning, but the Rockwells didn't seem to mind.

Pepper's irrepressible charm worked even through a tiny screen sending her image across the world. A few minutes later, she'd convinced Mr. Rockwell to fly out with Tyler and Sasha the following Friday, which happened to be the start of Labor Day weekend. Pepper used her phone to book their flights, as well as flights for that evening to New York for her and Eden, and to San Diego for Tyler.

By then, it was time for them to pack and head for the airport.

"I would drive you," Delta said, "but I don't think the pets would appreciate it. I've spent more time away from them in the past two days than I usually do in months."

They assured her it was all right, and got a cab.

Eden had never been in a plane before, or even in an airport. When they got there, she was surprised to see how hectic and confusing it was. Outside, people zig-zagged across the pavement, pulling suitcases on wheels or hefting duffel bags over their shoulders.

Once they entered through the sliding glass doors, counters stretched along the walls inside, below signs emblazoned with airline names. A line of impatient-looking mortals snaked in front of each counter.

They had to pass through security, which was like what she'd done at the Empire State Building, but more complicated. Here, you had to take off your shoes and put them in a bin that rode down a conveyor belt to be X-rayed. People with computers had to take them out and place them in separate bins. Luckily, Eden only had her backpack.

But before they got to the belts and the bins, they

had to show their tickets and identification to security guards at the entrance. When Eden showed her passport, the young security guard did a double take. "Aren't you the girl everyone was looking for?" he asked.

Before they'd booked their flights, they'd checked to make sure Brightly followed through with his end of the agreement with Goldie. Sure enough, the morning news was dominated by Brightly's announcement that the search for Eden had been a hoax, and was over.

"Yes," Eden said to the security guard. "That's me."

"Wow!" he said. "So it was all a lie! Why would David Brightly make that up?"

Eden shook her head and smiled. "I guess you'd have to ask him."

After security, they had to say goodbye to Tyler.

Pepper stood on her tiptoes and hugged him. "It was a true pleasure to meet you, Tyler," she said. "Now, if you'll excuse me, I'm going to shop for some airplane reading in that store over there." She wiggled her eyebrows at Eden as she left them alone.

Eden and Tyler stood against a wall to be out of the way of the people rushing down the hall. Tyler shook his hair out of his face. "I hate saying goodbye to you," he said. "But at least this time I know I'm going to see you again."

Being this close to him made Eden dizzy. "I still can't believe you came all the way here," she said.

"I think I'd do anything for you." Tyler took her hands, and a shiver ran down her spine.

She swallowed. "I—"

But before she could say anything, he leaned forward and kissed her cheek, as close to her lips as possible without touching them. Blood rushed to her head, and her body throbbed with happiness. The world had gone all wobbly and wonderful.

She realized he was waiting anxiously to see her reaction. When she smiled, he broke into a big smile too. "Okay," he said. "I have to go. But I'll see you soon."

"Very soon," she agreed.

When they hugged, he kissed the side of her head where her hair met her face. Then he squeezed her hands one more time, turned, and went down the crowded hall. She watched his gray backpack as he disappeared into the masses. Just before she lost him, he turned one more time and waved.

When Eden joined Pepper in the shop, her guardian's arms were full of magazines and chocolate bars.

"Hey, kid," she said sunnily. "Anything you want to add to the stash?"

Eden grabbed a bag of gummy bears and a book of

crossword puzzles. She was sure her face was red as a cherry, but Pepper didn't say anything about it. Eden was grateful. She wanted to keep what had just happened locked inside her heart, the way she'd once kept memories of Earth.

After buying everything, they went to the assigned gate. Their flight was just beginning to board.

A few minutes later, Eden followed Pepper through a gray tunnel that led to the plane. Their seats were near the back. Pepper told Eden to take the window seat so she could watch the clouds outside.

"Is this plane smaller than normal?" Eden asked as she slid into it. Her knees nearly touched the back of the seat in front of her.

Pepper almost choked on her water because she was laughing so hard. "No, this is regular size," she said. "But I know exactly what you mean."

Once everyone had boarded, they were instructed to buckle their seat belts. The flight attendant did a safety demonstration, and finally, the plane started rolling forward. It accelerated faster and faster until it lifted clear off the ground.

Eden pressed her forehead against the window and watched Paris disappear beneath her. The plane rose through a layer of fluffy white cumulus clouds that obscured Earth's surface completely, and Eden settled back in her seat.

She frowned. In the back of her mind was an annoying nagging feeling.

She was utterly relieved to be on the way back to New York with Pepper, and the fact that Tyler and Sasha would be there soon made things even better.

And yet, she had the unsettling suspicion there was something she'd missed, or forgotten about.

"Pepper," Eden said.

"Mmm-hmm?" Pepper was absorbed in a magazine. Her hair was in a puff of a ponytail high on her head.

"Why do you think Jane Johnston left the lab last night? Up till then, she was Brightly's best friend."

Pepper closed her magazine, but kept a finger inside to hold her place. She pursed her lips. "I'm not sure, kiddo. Maybe she wasn't as good a friend as he thought."

"But she was so involved the whole time," Eden said. "You'd think she'd want to stay and see what happened."

"Maybe she got scared when things started going wrong for them," said Pepper. "It's tough to find friends who stay by your side when things get hard. You know?"

The flight attendant came by and gave Eden a Coke on ice and two bags of peanuts. Pepper returned to her magazine, but Eden couldn't shake her uneasy feeling.

There was another part of the night that she couldn't make sense of: Where was Heloise? Athena had spoken to her in the hotel room, and supposedly she was the one who unlocked all the doors so they (and later Tyler) could enter Brightly Tech. But when they got to the lab, no one had seen her—not even Sylvana.

At the Grand Hotel Paris, Violet had said that Heloise left the auction early too—but not with Sylvana and Brightly. Violet also said that Heloise had only been Electric for a year. She'd been absent for a hundred years, after a disagreement with Sylvana.

Eden turned to Pepper again, but her guardian was fast asleep. Eden climbed over her and the man in the aisle seat, then stood on her tiptoes to remove her leather backpack from the overhead compartment. She followed the narrow aisle back to the airplane bathroom.

Inside the tiny room, she closed the door and turned the dial to lock it, making sure the OCCUPIED light was on. She put the lid down on the toilet and sat on it, then pulled her parchment paper from the backpack and unrolled it. She spoke to the paper to record the message.

"Hi, Goldie. Hi, Xavier. Hey, I have a question. I know you don't like talking about this, but I think it might be important this time. Could you tell me what Heloise's thousandth wish was?" She bit her lip. "I know you'll probably say no, but I figured I'd ask."

Someone knocked urgently on the door.

"Just a second!" she said. Then, to her masters: "Gotta go. Bye."

She rolled up the parchment paper and squeezed it, sending it on its magical journey to the lamp.

Thirty-One

They got back to Pepper's apartment late that night, so Eden didn't discover the answer to her message until the next day when she unpacked her backpack. Pepper had gone out to buy groceries, so she was in the apartment alone. She sat on the bed and unrolled the parchment paper.

"Hello, Eden," Xavier said as his image came to life. "I didn't think I'd hear from you again so soon." Eden rolled her eyes.

"You're correct that we don't make it a practice to share genies' thousandth wishes. But you said it's important, and I'm inclined to believe you. So just this once, I'll tell you. Heloise wished for two powers: teleportation and transfiguration."

Teleportation meant Heloise could vanish from one location and instantly appear at another.

Transfiguration meant she could completely change her form, or the way she looked.

"I hope that helps," Xavier said. "Oh, and welcome home."

Eden's thoughts zoomed around in her head, crashing into each other like bumper cars. She closed her eyes to concentrate on fitting the pieces together correctly.

A few minutes later, Pepper burst through the door carrying a plastic bag in each hand. "Eden!" she exclaimed. "You'll never guess what I just saw!"

"I think Heloise and Jane Johnston are the same person," Eden blurted.

Pepper's eyes grew huge. She set the bags on the floor and took a step closer. "Why do you say that?"

"Xavier just told me that Heloise's thousandth wish was for the powers of teleportation and transfiguration. So she could have been switching bodies the whole time, going back and forth between being Heloise and being Jane—and also, between Electra and Brightly Tech. Plus, Heloise spoke to Athena on the phone and told us how to get into the lab, but she was actually never there. But Jane was." Eden took a breath. "Think about it. No one ever saw them both in the same place at the same time."

Pepper stared at her wordlessly.

"I know it sounds crazy," Eden said. "But maybe

the whole time Jane was getting close to Brightly, she was planning to use him and his technology to track down the lamp. Over the years, she learned how to manipulate him. Maybe she wanted to use him to get back at Sylvana for whatever happened between them a hundred years ago!"

Still, Pepper didn't say a word.

"Pepper? Are you okay?"

Pepper blinked.

"What is it?"

Pepper held up her phone. "I just saw this on the news tickers in Times Square."

The headline read: BRIGHTLY NAILED FOR TAX EVASION.

Below it was a photo of Brightly being handcuffed by officers in FBI jackets.

The article began:

On the heels of the announcement that the alleged kidnapping of his adopted daughter was a hoax, David Brightly has made headlines again. This time, the tech mogul has been busted for tax evasion. He was arrested late last night when he landed at New York's JFK Airport. Early reports indicate that one of his employees tipped off the FBI. Brightly was returning from Paris, where he's been working on a top secret project. Reportedly, he was on the way to his home in Silicon Valley.

While Brightly awaits trial, control of Brightly Tech and all its entities will be in the hands of the company's vice president, Jane Johnston.

"Tax evasion!" Eden lifted her eyes to meet Pepper's. "The FBI!"

"Can you believe it?" Pepper asked.

"No need to worry about him for a while," Eden said.

"But Jane's taking over Brightly Tech," Pepper said soberly.

"And one of his employees tipped off the authorities." Eden's heart was beating fast. "Pepper, do you think it was her? Maybe she was planning to get him in trouble all along so she could take over the company. Do you think it's possible?"

Pepper said nothing. But from the look on her face, Eden could tell that she thought it was very possible indeed.

"Should we be worried?" Eden asked. "Do you think Jane—I mean, Heloise—could cause more trouble for us, or for the lamp?"

Pepper didn't answer. Instead, she went to the window that faced 44th Street and looked outside.

"You know what?" She tossed her phone on the bed. "I need a break from that thing. It's a beautiful day, and we're in New York City. Let's go for a walk. What do you say, kid?"

As they walked down the stairs, Pepper hummed a familiar tune. After a few bars, Eden joined in.

The past few weeks had been the hardest and most exciting of her life. The only thing she could be sure of was that there was more to come.

More to learn. More wishes to grant. Most likely, more problems to solve.

Hopefully, more moments like the goodbye at the airport.

Those things would come, and she'd face them as they did.

But for now, it was enough to know that she was home in New York City with Pepper—here, on the street where they lived.

Acknowledgments

Thank you to my brilliant editor, Laura Schreiber, who believed in Eden and in me from the start. And to the rest of the team at Disney Hyperion, whose talents and attention have made these books come together in such a special way.

Thank you to Kevan Lyon, my wise and tenacious agent.

Thank you to Nicholas Cuccia for educating me about physics labs and plasma shields.

To Abena Boafo, my reliable source on the French language and life in Paris.

To the lady at the Sorbonne Library who kindly agreed to show me around when her shift was over.

To Laura Michelle Kelly: You inspire me greatly. I think anyone who knows you will see your sparkling presence in these pages.

Thank you to my wonderful friends. I'm endlessly grateful for your love, support, and encouragement.

Thank you to my family, which expanded in such a beautiful way this year. Mom and Dad, I can't thank you enough for giving me the freedom and the blessing to chase my dreams.

Thank you to my husband, Henry. You make me happier than I ever imagined I could be.

A massive thank-you to all the readers of *Eden's Wish*. Meeting you at schools, in bookstores, in libraries, and online has made this journey unbelievably special.

Finally, this novel is deeply indebted to the splendor of the cities where it's set. New York, I love you. Paris, *je t'aime*! Thank you for bringing so much magic to the world.